Exiled
– to the –
Red River

Trailblazer Books

*Hero Tales: A Family Treasury of True Stories
From the Lives of Christian Heroes* (Volumes I, II, III, & IV)

*Curriculum guide available.
Written by Julia Pferdehirt with Dave & Neta Jackson.

03C

Exiled
– to the –
Red River

Dave & Neta Jackson

Illustrated by Anne Gavitt

BETHANY HOUSE PUBLISHERS
MINNEAPOLIS, MINNESOTA 55438

Exiled to the Red River
Copyright © 2003
Dave and Neta Jackson

Illustrations © 2003
Bethany House Publishers

Story illustrations by Anne Gavitt.
Cover design and illustration by Catherine Reishus McLaughlin.

Scripture quotations are from the King James Version of the Bible.

Published by Bethany House Publishers
11400 Hampshire Avenue South
Bloomington, Minnesota 55438
www.bethanyhouse.com

Bethany House Publishers is a Division of
Baker Book House Company, Grand Rapids, Michigan.

Printed in the United States of America

Library of Congress Cataloging-in-Publication Data

CIP Data applied for

ISBN 0–7642–2235–X

We tell the stories in our other thirty-nine TRAIL-BLAZER BOOKS from the perspective of a young person who *encounters* the adult hero featured in the book. In this book, however, the main character *is* the hero of the book because Chief Spokane Garry's incredible ministry and contributions were largely accomplished while he was still a teenager, either sixteen or eighteen years of age.

In addition to dramatizing various details, we have departed from known facts in the following respects: In 1822, Fort Gibraltar's name was changed to Fort Garry. We, however, retained its earlier name to avoid confusion with our hero's name.

Because we do not know the name of the Red River teacher who worked most closely with Garry and Pelly, we have called him Arnold Worthington. Similarly, we gave the man from the Hudson's Bay Company at Fort Assiniboine the name of Captain McKay.

Pelly's horse accident did not occur on his trip home but after he arrived back among his people. His injuries were severe, but he still returned with Garry to the Red River Mission in the spring of 1830 to deliver five more young men—all the sons of chiefs—for Christian training. It was while in Red River, at the home of Rev. Jones on Easter, 1831, that he succumbed to his injuries.

Finally, Garry learned of his father's death before leaving the Red River Mission, probably in the spring of 1828, by way of trappers returning from the Columbia region, rather than after he arrived home.

Find us on the Web at . . .

TrailblazerBooks.com

- Meet the authors.

- Read the first chapter of each book—with the pictures.

- Track the Trailblazers around the world on a map.

- Use the historical timeline to find out what other important events were happening in the world at the time of each Trailblazer story.

- Discover how the authors research their books, and link to some of the same sources they used, where you can learn more about these heroes.

- Write to the authors.

- Explore frequently asked questions about writing and Trailblazer books.

> **LIMITED OFFER:**
> *Arrange for Dave and Neta Jackson to come to your school or homeschool group for a one- or two-day writing seminar.*

Just point your browser to *www.trailblazerbooks.com*.

CONTENTS

DAVE AND NETA JACKSON are a full-time husband and wife writing team who have authored and coauthored many books. Their books for children include the TRAILBLAZER series and *Hero Tales,* volumes I, II, III, and IV. The Jacksons make their home in Evanston, Illinois.

Chapter 1

Circling Raven's Prophecy

Like a dank fog, the sickness crept from lodge to lodge through the whole village. Even in the other villages and other tribes on the Columbia Plateau, which was cupped between the Rocky Mountains and the Cascades, both women and children, old people and great warriors had died from the smallpox in 1782. Those who had recovered displayed rough scars on their faces as though they had done battle with the great porcupine.

But Circling Raven, the shaman, or prophet, among the Spokane people, had faith that *Quilent-sat-men*, the Creator of All, would hear his prayers and send healing. Maybe a few evil people would die, but the great God Most High certainly would save those who worshiped Him and lived a righteous life.

Quiet moaning like the winter wind threading its way through the pines seeped from young Chief Illim-Spokanee's lodge as Circling Raven approached it. The lodge was fifty feet long and fifteen wide, made of limber poles bent in a series of arches and covered with buffalo hides and tightly woven mats of tule reeds.

He tossed back the door flap and stepped in, then stood still for a few moments to allow his eyes to adjust to the dim light coming through the smoke holes in the roof. In the far corner, bending over a sleeping mat, he made out the forms of three women. Suddenly the moaning erupted into a wail of trilling agony that Circling Raven knew was the death cry. Had he come too late? No evil people lived in *this* lodge. The chief and all his relatives were good people, but as he drew nearer, he saw that the sickness had taken the chief's mother.

She was an older woman, about the same age as Circling Raven. Maybe it was her time, but Circling Raven didn't feel like *his* years were over. He tried to comfort the family by praying long and loudly that God would receive the woman's spirit. But even as he prayed, doubts bubbled up inside him like the pungent sulfur water from the hot springs. If God did not hear his prayers and drive away the sickness, how could he believe that God would answer his prayers that the dead would find the path to heaven?

That evening at council, Two Claws, a brash young brave, said, "My woman thinks evil spirits have come to live along the Spokane River and Circling Raven's medicine is not strong enough to drive them away. She says we should move the village."

Circling Raven did not answer. He did not even look up from watching the trail of red ants that marched past his foot. The Spokane people were semi-nomadic, so the idea of moving was not unusual, but this spot along the river, just below the falls, had been a favorite campground year after year. The idea of giving it up because it was unfit would be like abandoning one's mother.

"Where would we go?" asked Chief Illim-Spokanee. "All the tribes have the sickness."

"We could go to the lands of the Blackfeet," said Two Claws. He laughed. "Then we could hunt buffalo whenever we pleased."

"And die at the hands of the Blackfeet," said Chief Illim-Spokanee.

Two Claws snorted. "You sound like a white rabbit. We have at least a thousand people and many braves. We could defend ourselves."

"You are too young to remember anything more than the raiding parties the Blackfeet send to harass us when we enter their lands to hunt the buffalo. But they are a powerful nation."

"Perhaps they have only a few braves, just enough for some raiding parties."

"You are too young," agreed one of the older chiefs.

"And you are old—maybe too old," snorted Two

Claws. He kept trying to talk of leaving the camp beside the river, but no one paid attention.

No one, that is, except Circling Raven. The shaman began to wonder whether Two Claws might be right—though not about leaving the Spokane. He knew moving would not protect them, but maybe his medicine was weak. As the days went by, he prayed harder, but the villagers continued to die. Did God no longer care about them?

Then came the day when Circling Raven's own son got sick. Circling Raven prayed all night. He helped his wife nurse the small eight-year-old, cooling the child's fevered brow with a damp deerskin rag and singing softly to him when the boy cried out in his restless sleep. Two days went by, then three, but the fever did not leave the lad until early one morning when it stole the boy's spirit right out of his body, and he was no more.

Circling Raven ripped the flap off the door to his lodge as he ran out. "Why? Why? Why?" He shook his fist at the sky. "If the righteous die while evil men live, why should we continue to follow our laws? Let us live like the animals! Why care about God?" He began tearing down the wooden racks that held the drying salmon over smoking beds of coals. "Here, brother dogs, eat our fish," he yelled, tossing a fish to the dogs that were barking at his wild antics. "And when the winter comes we will eat you. What difference does it make? Or maybe we will eat each other and simply die like dogs!"

Chief Illim-Spokanee came out of his lodge and

watched Circling Raven vent his rage and grief until the shaman fell to the ground exhausted and began to weep, not caring whether the other men of the village thought him an old woman. Then the chief came and sat down beside the older prophet. He rocked back and forth like a sapling swaying in the breeze, humming a mournful chant in tune with the shaman's broken heart. The chief stayed with him until the sun was high overhead, and then he said, "My brother, you must not give up your faith. You have just lost your way because of the sickness. It may not be killing your body, but your spirit has the fever."

Circling Raven threw a handful of dust in the air. "I no longer believe in God."

"Then why do you yell at Him? Do you yell at the wind? Do you yell at the trees? No. They cannot hear you. But you yell at God, so I do not think you have lost your faith altogether." The chief put his hand gently on the shaman's shoulder. "Take some time, my older brother; take some time. Climb Mount Spokane and pray and fast. See if you can't revive your spirit before it becomes twisted like the lone pine tree on Pine Bluff."

Circling Raven thought about the chief's words. He could feel his spirit becoming gnarled and ugly like the lightning-blazed pine. He nodded his head. "I will go. I will go to the mountain and pray until God hears me or until I die crying out to Him. For what other reason is there to live if He does not hear our cry and uphold us?"

The next morning, Circling Raven arose before dawn and prepared for his journey to Mount Spokane. His wife handed him a leather pouch of pemmican and smoked salmon, but Circling Raven waved it away and left the village without a word.

He had walked forty-five miles by the time he arrived at the peak of Mount Spokane the next afternoon. He was the only human on the mountain, and even though snow still lay on the ground and he had no buffalo robe, he did not feel the cold as he sat in the mouth of a shallow cave. Instead of seeking his own comfort, he cried out, "O *Quilent-sat-men*, Great God Most High, Creator of All, why have you forsaken your people, the Spokane? If we have displeased you, if we have sinned against you in any way, please forgive us. If I have offended you with my yelling, if I have broken any of your laws, please forgive me."

For four days and four nights, Circling Raven fasted and prayed in this manner. And then . . . God gave him a vision, a vision as big as the sky.

A voice rolled back and forth between the clouds like thunder. "Why do you cry? Your son is happy here with me, so you should have faith." In the vision, Circling Raven saw his own lodge with smoke coming out of all three roof holes. Healthy children ran around the village without scars on their faces, and in the meadow by the Spokane River, young boys raced their horses and made bets on who could ride faster. And then he saw two men get out of a canoe. They wore strange clothes and had white

skin. In their hands they carried a pack of leaves
bound together and wrapped in black leather. God's
voice crackled: "Pay attention to the marks on those
leaves. They are the Leaves of Life."

Circling Raven leaped to his feet and started to
run down the mountain, so excited about the vision
that he tripped over roots and rocks in his path so
many times that his hands and knees were bloody
when he arrived at the village. He did not wait to call
a council meeting but blurted out his report, describ-
ing the vision even though only women and children

gathered to hear him. Finally one of the old chiefs interrupted and urged him to come into the council lodge and allow time for the other chiefs and elders to gather.

When all had assembled, they listened to Circling Raven's report and passed the pipe from one to another. But Circling Raven did not tell the last part of his vision, the part about the sad things that would happen later when more white men followed the first few who carried the Leaves of Life. He did not want to frighten his people.

When the prophet finished his report, everyone nodded and passed the pipe around the circle. It went around twice until the oldest chief said, "Could this prophecy be similar to the one given by Shining Shirt to our neighbors, the Salish? They call God *Amotkan,* He Who Lives on Most High. But I think they worship *Quilent-sat-men* just as we do. They just know Him by a different name. Shining Shirt said to pray to God every day and do only what is right and honest, and someday men with pale skins and long black shirts would come from the East and teach the truth."

There was silence as the pipe went around the circle again. "This is good," some muttered. "We should pray every day, too. We should obey God's instruction." They continued to pass the pipe from one to the other and stared into the fire until only a few glowing coals remained. Then one by one they slipped out of the council lodge and walked to their own homes, careful not to awaken the children as they crawled into their buffalo robes.

The next day they assured their people that Circling Raven had received a true vision. God was good, and He had not forgotten them even though many still suffered from the sickness.

In time, the smallpox epidemic passed, and life in the Spokane nation returned to its normal routine of hunting, fishing, gathering, and horse racing. Even though Circling Raven still missed the son he lost to the sickness, he was able to grow old peacefully and take joy in the healthy children born to his relatives, and in this way his lodge became full again so that smoke rose from all three holes in the roof. Always at the tribal council he urged his people to live righteous lives of honesty and faith in the Creator and to pray daily for His blessing.

And then one day the earth shook and the sky became dark, and dry snow began to fall from the heavens. It covered the grass and the rocks. It caught in the people's noses and made their eyes burn so that they had to sip water continually to keep from coughing, and they had to calm their horses so they would not stampede.

The year was 1800, and the dry snow was ash from the volcanic eruption of the Smoking Mountain (later called Mount St. Helens), hundreds of miles to the west where fire dragons lived. The Spokane people began to cry and tremble. "The world is ending! The world is ending! Everything is lost!"

Circling Raven, however, remembered his vision. "People, people, do not fear. This is not the end," he said as he gathered the people together in the choking cloud of dust. "This cannot be the end because the white men have not come yet."

Slowly they calmed down. He was, after all, a good prophet who had always encouraged them to live a righteous life. Again he reminded them of his vision and pointed out how some of it had already come true. Their tribe had recovered from the sickness and was prospering in every way. God was good!

But he felt badly that he had not had the courage to tell his whole vision. So he cleared his throat and said, "There was one more part to my vision. After the white men come with their Leaves of Life that show us the path to heaven, our lives will change in ways we cannot even imagine. They will show us new ways to make a living, and all wars between us will cease."

A murmur of approval spread through the crowd as various people coughed to clear their throats. Circling Raven held up his hand, indicating he had more to say. "This has not yet happened, so the world cannot be ending. However, after the white men with the Leaves of Life come, other white men will come who will make slaves of us. Then our world will end, but not with ashes. We will simply be overrun by the white men as though by grasshoppers. When this happens, we should not fight as it would only create unnecessary bloodshed."

The people were silent, except for occasional coughing. Slowly and by family groups, they went back to their lodges. Maybe, thought some, if they could just get the Leaves of Life, they could please God and He would spare them from being overrun by the white men. Maybe they could learn to live together in peace with the white men.

Chapter 2

The Salmon Run

Eleven winters after the "dry snow," a child was born in the tent of Chief Illim-Spokanee. Later he would be called Spokane Garry. The baby's mother died giving him birth, so even though he had several older brothers and sisters, he would be the last son of the chief, the baby in the family. His siblings cared for him as best they could, but it was never like growing up with a loving mother, dedicated to meeting his every need.

In 1806, five years before the child was born, three Spokane braves had been down the Snake River where they had met white men traveling from the east in large canoes. Their leaders were called

Lewis and Clark. So it was true, the braves said when they returned, that such pale-skinned people existed, and there was even a black man among them.

And about the time Garry was born, white men actually came to Spokane country, just as Circling Raven had prophesied, but they had not brought the Leaves of Life. Instead, they built a big log trading post on the flat land just above where the Little Spokane flows into the Spokane River. The white traders were named Finan McDonald—a tall man with blue eyes—and Jacob Finlay, a shorter man who was part Indian.

Could these men with pale faces be the ones to fulfill Circling Raven's prophecy? Just in case, Chief Illim moved his lodge to a site just across the river from the white men's trading post where he could wait and watch, even though he knew that the spring rains sometimes flooded the flats on both sides of the river. Other Indians followed Illim's example until a new village formed on the site. Day after day, as little Garry toddled around the camp, the old chief sat in front of his lodge and watched the white men across the river, but he never saw them pray or worship.

From time to time, Chief Illim went over to the trading post and sat around, asking the white men about what they knew of God, but they only waved a hand in dismissal and changed the subject. "How about trading some of your old dried-out salmon or mangy furs or even a horse for some of these sharp knives and bright beads that we brought? After all, you don't need all those horses." Chief Illim traded when it pleased him and walked away with a grunt when it didn't, but he suspected that the white men knew more about God than they admitted, so he watched.

As the seasons passed into years, young Spokane Garry grew strong and daring, always trying to do whatever his older brothers and sisters were doing. Before he could walk without stumbling, he tried to climb the stately ponderosa pine trees around the village. When other children his age were making mud pies along the riverbank, he waded into the clear pools to chase the elusive trout. When he should have been content to play tag with the dogs in the village, he tried to find a stump to stand on so he could climb onto the back of a pony. And with every new thing, the other children followed. His father nodded in satisfaction. "He will make a great chief someday."

Tribes from around the area called the trading post "Spokane House," and the goods they brought to trade made the Spokane tribe, as well as the white men, rich. But wealth did not satisfy the old chief. He was looking for God, and so in the evenings, around the fire, he told the old stories to keep alive the hope of his people.

Little Garry was always a ready listener. "Father, tell us about the Leaves of Life that the white men were supposed to bring," he often begged. But after Chief Illim recited the old prophecies, the other men around the fire wanted to talk about whether their world would soon come to an end now that the white men had come. Once, an Indian from the great water far to the west, beyond the smoking mountain where the fire dragons lived, stopped at their village. He said he had seen many palefaces. They came from across the sea in great canoes with white wings, but they were only interested in trading for furs and did not build villages or even a log house like the trading post.

Everyone nodded and leaned back in relief. If the white men were not building villages, then they were not planning to stay and therefore couldn't be too dangerous . . . at least not yet.

In 1824, when Garry was thirteen years old, he decided that he definitely wanted to go on the buffalo hunt that fall. The trip east to the land of the Blackfeet was dangerous, and only able-bodied warriors and the strongest women were allowed to go. Garry knew the Blackfeet might attack at any time. But if he could kill a buffalo, that would prove he was a man.

Every day the boy went hunting across the river, climbing the steep crags of Lookout Mountain. Sometimes he stayed out two or three days until he shot a deer to bring back to camp to demonstrate what a good hunter he was becoming.

When Garry was not hunting, he rode one of his father's horses, wheeling it right and left as he raced across the meadow like a hummingbird darting from flower to flower while he clung to its bare back and drove his lance into the rotten stumps in the middle of the field. There was no doubt that he was skilled and strong, but could he kill a buffalo?

One day a new trader arrived at Spokane House, a man named Alexander Ross of the Hudson's Bay Company. In trade for the salmon and furs the Indians brought to him, he offered hunting sticks called rifles that could kill a bear at two hundred paces, steel traps that could catch the beaver in ponds without having to wait and watch, and warm blankets that were lighter and more colorful than the heavy buffalo robes. But the rifles were the prize! They would ensure a successful buffalo hunt and provide certain protection against the Blackfeet.

But in July, all the hunting stopped as the whole tribe prepared for the run of the red sockeye salmon up the Spokane River. The old traps were repaired and new willow baskets were woven. When the fish began fighting their way upstream, young and old went to the falls where the women set up their drying racks, and the men repaired the fishing platforms that stood precariously out over the swirling white water. Then they worked day and night catching, cleaning, and smoking the fish. Salmon were not only a prime source of food for the tribe, but they had become a great trading item with the whites and with other tribes that did not live on a river.

At dusk one evening, when the hills along the river were no more than silhouettes against the twilight glow of the blue-jay sky and the bonfires crackling along the shore, Chief Illim said to Garry, "Take a canoe down to Spokane House and ask Mr. Ross for four new knives. Some of the old ones are wearing out, and women need new ones to clean and cut the fish. Tell him we'll pay him what's fair later."

Garry was grateful to get off the shaky platform where the cold mist from the falls soaked him like a fall rain. He was so tired and his legs so numb that he could hardly keep his footing. It was only a mile to the trading post, but if he took his time, it would be dark before he returned. Maybe by then his father would tell everyone to take a rest. Garry couldn't imagine how such an old man could work day and night without a break.

Once away from the falls, the river smoothed out to reflect the sky. The roll of an occasional salmon disturbed its glassy surface, and sometimes Garry bumped one of the determined submarines with his paddle.

Bullfrogs trumpeted from the tules along the shore, and a muskrat swam to the middle of the river, turned, and drew a V that guided Garry downstream. Once around the gentle bend where the boy could see the white man's smoke thread its way straight up from the stone chimney of Spokane House, he spotted two strange canoes pulled up on the beach near the trading post. They were not Indian canoes.

He wanted to turn around immediately and paddle upriver to tell his father, but he had little to tell—only that strangers had come to the trading post. Drifting with the current, he silently approached the log house, nosing his canoe into a hiding place among some willows above the beach where the strangers' canoes sat, still piled high with supplies.

Garry climbed out and cautiously approached the building. From within he heard uproarious laughter and the strange words of the white man's tongue. At first he was afraid to go in, but his father would be wanting the knives. And he was curious. Who were these strangers? Summoning his courage, he pushed open the door.

"Ah, see here!" shouted Alexander Ross. "I have not scared 'em off. Here's one of the chief's whelps right now. Come in, boy, before a bear follers ya."

Garry stepped in and closed the heavy plank door, thick enough indeed to keep bears out if they caught a whiff of the trader's bacon and maple sugar. In the dim light cast by a small fire and a couple of oil lamps, he saw two dusty trappers, elbows on the table while they shoveled some kind of stew into their mouths. They glanced up at Garry only long enough to note that he was there before holding their bowls out to Ross, who stood to the side ready to serve more of the steaming mix from a large black pot.

"These here men are straight from Hudson's Bay Company," Ross said to Garry. "They tell me that Governor George Simpson of the Northern Division will be coming by here next spring—he's a big chief

in the company—and your pa will want to parlay with him. Think you can remember to tell 'im all that?"

"Yes, sir," said Garry.

"Good, 'cause your father keeps pestering me 'bout religion, but Governor Simpson is the man who can tell him everything he'll ever want to know about God. Am I right, Jeb?" One of the trappers grunted as he put down his spoon and raised the stew bowl to his mouth to slurp in the contents faster. "So you tell the chief that," added Mr. Ross.

Garry nodded and backed toward the door. He

kept nodding as he opened the door and left. In the gloom of the late twilight, he ran toward his canoe and headed upriver, paddling hard.

It was not until he saw the fires of the salmon camp that he remembered he had not gotten the knives his father had sent him to get.

Chapter 3

"Take a Hundred Children"

But, Father, you *can't* say no," moaned Garry as he stood before his father outside their lodge. "I've been counting on this. I'm old enough. I'm ready. I'm a good hunter!"

Chief Illim-Spokanee sat on the old buffalo hide as though he were a stone, the weathered skin on his face sagging like melting beeswax. Even the wisp of smoke that blew into his watery eyes from the ashes of the morning fire did not cause him to blink. Finally he spoke. "You are becoming a good hunter, but I cannot let you go, my son. You are my youngest, my child of promise from the time of the great sickness. I cannot risk the Blackfeet killing you on the buffalo hunt."

"But if that's how you feel, you'll never let me go!"

As a young child, Garry had always loved hearing about the old days, how God had saved their people from being wiped out by the sickness and the prophecies spoken by Circling Raven about the leaves that would tell the way to heaven. But lately it seemed his father could think of nothing else, as though his only reason for living was to see the fulfillment of the prophecy. "Maybe next spring when the great white chief, George Simpson, comes . . ." he would say, no matter what the subject was, as though the whole world waited on that visit. Garry regretted ever telling his father the news brought by the white trappers during the summer's salmon run.

Now it was time for the tribe to go east on their fall buffalo hunt, and his father wouldn't let him go. Garry crossed his arms and straightened his lean body to its full height. "I will soon be a man, Father, and then you will not be able to stop me!" He cringed at making such a defiant threat, but he didn't care if it angered his father or not. Keeping him home just wasn't fair, especially not after . . . "I've hunted all summer except during the salmon run, and I've probably brought in as much game as any other man. And you know I can ride as well as—"

He talked on, hoping to soften the defiant challenge he had made to his father, but the chief addressed it directly. "I hope it doesn't come to that, my son. I hope you will honor me even when you don't have to."

Garry let out the air he'd sucked into his lungs and dropped his arms, but his lips tightened into a straight line as he turned and stomped away, not caring whether the dust he kicked up drifted back over his father.

It wasn't fair, and he would find some way to show his father how angry he was. It would be childish to simply refuse to speak to his father. On the other hand, what did they have to talk about?—certainly not the buffalo hunt, and Garry was getting so he didn't care anymore about Governor George Simpson's coming.

But as the day approached when the tribe would leave for the hunt, Garry realized that, for the first time, his father wasn't going, either. Was his father really getting that old? Chief Illim's face was wrinkled and his fingers twisted, but he was still strong, and he could ride like the wind with his long gray hair flying out behind him.

"It is time to attend to other things, like prayer," Garry overheard the chief say to his uncle. "You will do fine without me, especially with those new rifles."

So, thought Garry miserably, it will be just the chief, the old women and children, and me left back here in the village. Well, he would just spend more time out hunting so he wouldn't have to be with his father any more than necessary.

On the morning the buffalo hunters rode out of the village, Garry had already hiked high on Lookout Mountain. He blinked back tears of anger and disappointment as he watched the trail of ponies and riders snake across the meadow, still white with the season's first hard frost. He should pray for their success, but he could not bring himself to do so. He didn't want them coming back with great stories from the hunt—the hunt that should have been his first. That would be too much.

When the hunters returned three weeks later, however, they arrived without any glorious hunting stories. Instead, they brought back the bodies of three dead warriors, shot by Blackfeet raiding parties that also had rifles now. As for meat, they had killed only six buffalo, hardly enough to feed the village through the winter, and certainly not enough for new robes to protect them from the cold. "It's a good thing the white traders have blankets," some of the women grumbled.

That night Garry sat on his haunches in the shadows as the council discussed the disheartening hunt. The three dead Spokane braves had been shot on the same day. Two were killed immediately, and though the other one had clung to life for several days, his life finally drifted away like a wisp of smoke on the morning breeze.

"Our hunting ways must change. We must post lookouts for Blackfeet raiders as well as send out scouts to find the herds."

"The herds we did find seemed smaller and more scattered."

"The Blackfeet are taking more than their share of the buffalo!"

But Garry's uncle disagreed. "A Nez Perce warrior told me that white buffalo hunters have been chasing the herds all summer long and killing far more than they could possibly eat. The Nez Perce had seen piles of rotting carcasses."

Angry murmurs circled the council ring. How would the tribe survive with enemies on every side making it difficult to hunt the buffalo?

Garry crept away before the council broke up. He didn't want to face his father after hearing about the hunters who had been shot. His father would use it to prove he had been right all along and there *had* been good reason to keep him home. "Huh!" Garry muttered to himself. "Just because they were shot doesn't mean that I would have been killed. I would have been more cautious." When he hunted on Lookout Mountain, he sometimes had to climb dangerous cliffs to get into a good position. "Hunting's always dangerous. I could be thrown off a horse and hit my head just riding through camp. Father is too protective! He just won't let me grow up!"

Throughout the winter, Garry held on to his grudge toward his father, talking to him only when necessary just to make sure his father knew how angry he was for not letting him go on the buffalo hunt. From time to time, Garry imagined that his anger might convince his father that he had made a mistake. But he knew he could not manipulate the wise old chief so easily. If Chief Illim still thought it was wrong to let his son go on the hunt, Garry could be as angry as a stirred-up wasps' nest, and though his father would be sad that their relationship was strained, it would not force him to change his mind.

"He is a chief, after all," muttered Garry as he threw a snowball at a squirrel, "not a reed to be swayed by the wind."

Mail traveled remarkably fast in the wilderness, passed from trapper to trapper until Alexander Ross received a letter from Governor George Simpson of the Northern Division of the Hudson's Bay Company. Simpson had spent the winter at Fort George at the mouth of the Columbia River, but he planned to arrive at Spokane House in early April, depending, of course, on the snow in the passes and how high the rivers were. "I would like to speak to the important chiefs in the area if you can arrange for them to meet me at your trading post," the letter said. "The Reverend David T. Jones gave me an assignment that I hope to carry out."

When Ross told Chief Illim of Simpson's request, the old chief nodded solemnly. "I will send word to all the Spokane chiefs and invite our neighboring tribes to attend the powwow, as well," he promised.

When the snow on the mountains began to melt and its gurgling water broke up the ice in the streams, Chief Illim asked Garry to sit with him by his fire in the lodge. It was the first time the chief had asked his son to talk with him in such a formal way.

"I need someone to visit all the Spokane villages

to tell them
about the coming of this white
man," said the old chief. "Do you want to go?"

Garry hesitated. "Me? At this time of year?" It would take at least three days with the trails still treacherous with ice.

"Choose someone to go with you if you want."

Garry realized the request was a statement of his father's respect for his horsemanship and responsibility, not something he would ask a child to do. But still, clinging to his internal winter, Garry answered coolly, "Why?"

The chief's eyebrows went up, and he stared at his son for a few moments. "Any good brave can hunt buffalo"—he had not forgotten what caused the tension between them—"but this has to do with your purpose in life."

Purpose in life? What did that mean? Did his father really think being an errand boy was more important than proving he was a man? "Send someone else," he said and got up and walked out of the lodge.

To Garry's surprise, his father did not insist, and later that afternoon he saw one of the young braves ride out of the village on the mission his father had offered him.

Three weeks later, the other Spokane chiefs began to gather. In addition, delegations from neighboring tribes arrived, too, especially from the Nez Perce and various Flathead nations. Garry noticed a boy about his age with a Kootenai chief, but since he could not understand the language, he didn't try to make friends. But his father seemed able to communicate adequately with everyone, filling in with sign language when words eluded him.

Then one day, two large wooden boats with several white men pulling on the oars rowed slowly upriver until they beached at Spokane House. The brigade of fur traders had also come to meet Governor

George Simpson, who arrived on horseback from the south in the afternoon on April 8, 1825.

Garry feigned only slight interest as the visitors set up their tepees on the meadow between the Spokane village and the river in preparation for the powwow. Eight regal chiefs strutted about in their finest fur-lined ceremonial dress and stately feathered headbands, along with many warriors and leading women. As game roasted over open fires, the white men came across the river, and the festivities began with dancing and feasting and constant displays of horsemanship.

Garry could not resist the horse races. No sooner was one horse race over than someone proposed another. The white men freely bet on who would win each race, putting up a knife or a hatchet or some other valuable item. After winning most of the events he entered, Garry went up behind his father and tapped him on the shoulder. Pointing at Governor Simpson, he said, "Tell the white chief that I can beat anyone in a race to the top of Pine Bluff, around the lone pine, and back down here to the camp if he will put up his rifle as prize." Garry pointed to the gnarled old pine tree on the top of the ridge to the south and then to Simpson's gun so that it was clear what he wanted.

The governor seemed amused. "He wants to race for my rifle?"

Alexander Ross, who knew the Spokane language better, confirmed the challenge. Governor Simpson nodded thoughtfully, looking back and forth between

Garry, Chief Illim, and the Kootenai boy, who was obviously interested in participating. Finally he said, "Tell the boy and the chiefs that it's a deal—provided they will let me have those two boys to take to our headquarters in Canada." He pointed directly at Garry and at the Kootenai chief's son.

"What?" roared Garry's father, understanding enough of the white man's speech to get the message. "Do you think we are dogs that we would give up our children for you to take them"—he stuttered, his face getting red—"take them who knows where?" He stood up, whipping his blanket around him like a cocoon.

"Wait! Wait!" said Alexander Ross. "I'm sure the governor did not mean any insult. Now, Chief, you are always asking me about religion, about the Bible . . . you know, the book you call the Leaves of Life. Well, that's all the governor is saying. He's offering to take your son—young Garry here and that Kootenai boy—to study religion at the best Indian school in Canada." Taking a breath, he quickly told Simpson what he had said in Spokane, since the governor's abilities in that language were limited.

"Yes." The governor stood up. "I want to take a couple of your bright young boys to learn how to know and serve God. Then, after four winters, they can come back here and tell all your people what they've learned."

Chief Illim relaxed slightly. "You would teach my boy about *Quilent-sat-men?*"

"*Quilent-sat-men?*" Simpson frowned at Ross.

"Their word for God. It means Creator of All."

Simpson faced the chief while talking to Ross. "Of course! I would take them to Rev. Jones at the missionary school, and there he would learn about God." Simpson pointed up. "God . . . your *Quil*-something-or-other, whatever you call Him."

The chief's face froze, and then his head nodded ever so slightly. "If you will teach them about God, you can take a hundred of our children." He spoke quickly to the other chiefs in their various languages, and they began nodding vigorously. The Kootenia chief pushed his son forward, and Garry could see that he was even younger than himself.

Chief Illim sat down—as did Simpson and all the other chiefs in a ring around the main fire. Chief Illim drew out his pipe and began to fill it with tobacco.

"What about my horse race?" hissed Garry in his father's ear. "I want to win that rifle!"

"Don't worry about it, son," said the chief over his shoulder. "You will be the greatest chief our people have ever known—not by winning a horse race or killing buffalo, but by bringing home the Leaves of Life!"

Chapter 4

Exiled to the Red River

Garry stepped back and his mouth went dry. He had been so interested in winning the governor's rifle that he had not paid very close attention to what the men were discussing—something about sending children somewhere . . . to school—whatever that was—in Canada, for four years?

His father had said bringing home the Leaves of Life would make him a great chief, but that didn't make sense. His father had not allowed him to go on the buffalo hunt; then Garry had refused to do his father's errand. Now his father was sending him far away to a place called Red River. It *felt* more like a punishment.

He was being exiled, taken away by these white men. And where was Canada? Somewhere north was all he knew.

He looked over at the Kootenai boy. His father was down on his knee in front of the boy talking very earnestly while the boy kept shaking his head like a bear with a salmon in its mouth. Tears were coming into the boy's eyes, and his face was screwing up as though he had eaten green berries.

Garry turned away. Whatever was happening, he would not cry. He walked swiftly to the horse corral, led out his favorite paint horse, and climbed on. Without thinking about what he was doing, he let his horse gallop across the meadow and up the steep hill that bordered it on the southwest and headed toward the twisted figure of the old lightning-blazed tree on the top of Pine Bluff.

Once over the crest of the plateau, he kept on riding, telling himself that the tears streaming back from his eyes were only from the cold wind. He let his horse slow to a walk and find its own way for the next couple miles, weaving around small ponds, following game trails through the underbrush, until he arrived at a burial platform. On top of the platform, Garry knew that the bones of his mother rested, wrapped tightly in old animal skins, maybe little more than dust by now. And yet he felt some comfort in her memory and in what he imagined she would have been like to know.

From time to time, he had asked his older sisters and brothers about Mother. His next oldest brother,

Sultz-lee, wouldn't even answer his questions, and the descriptions of his other siblings were short, almost angry, as though he had no right to ask. She had died giving him birth was all they would tell him. Did that mean it was his fault? He sometimes felt like it. But he didn't think she would have blamed him. That's just not what a mother would do.

Garry slid off the paint and sat with his back against one of the poles of the platform, his weight causing it to wiggle and shake some dust down on his head. His mind drifted to what lay ahead—a long trip to a place he didn't know with people who spoke a strange language. He shivered . . . was it a gust of wind off the snow-capped mountains or the draft of cold loneliness swirling in his heart? He tried to think back four years to when he was ten. Being sent away for that much longer seemed like forever. He didn't want to go. And yet, he knew it would happen.

Why was his father sending *him*? Why didn't he go himself if he wanted to learn to know God? And what was all this talk about it making him a great chief? What if he couldn't find the Leaves of Life and bring them back to his people? What if he failed? This wouldn't be like a buffalo hunt where if you didn't kill one of the great beasts one year, you could go back and try again the next.

He looked up at the platform, wishing he could talk to his mother. But of course that wasn't possible. This was something he was going to have to do on his own . . . but he wished he had someone wise to talk to.

A loud cry yanked him from the journey he was imagining in his mind, and he looked up just as a large black bird glided to a perch on top of his mother's burial platform. It cawed as though scolding him. Garry scrambled to his feet. "This is my mother's platform, not yours!" he yelled, tossing a stick at the bird. The large bird swooped off the platform and sailed off between the pines.

"A raven," he muttered—and as soon as he said

it, he thought of his long-dead uncle, Circling Raven. *When he felt alone he prayed to God,* thought Garry. *But he was a shaman, a prophet, and I am only a boy.* Garry continued to look through the trees in the direction the raven had flown. Suddenly the bird rose above the treetops and began circling higher and higher on an updraft.

"Oh, God, if you can hear me, if you will listen to a mere boy, help me to be brave about being sent away! And if you are there, bring me back home safely!"

Garry stood, head back and arms thrown out, as the wind seemed to snatch his words and hurl them upward, like the raven. Then quietness settled back over the forest and, strangely, into his spirit, as well.

Grabbing the reins of his paint, Garry began walking back to the village. Something had changed. Even as he walked, the chill of fear receded like the memory of last night's dream, while eagerness warmed within him to see this Red River—even if he was being exiled. But what had changed? Had his simple prayer made the difference? Had God heard him? The possibility excited him. He vaulted onto his horse and kicked him into a run.

Four days later, Governor Simpson was ready to leave. The water level in the river had dropped because there had been no rain, so it wasn't safe to load the two wooden boats with supplies and passengers;

they might smash on underwater rocks. Simpson chose four men to launch each boat and head downriver. The rest of the brigade, along with the two chiefs' sons, would travel by horseback—borrowed from the Spokane tribe—down to the junction of the Spokane with the Columbia. There the water would be deep enough to load passengers and supplies into the boats. The plan, Chief Illim told his son, was to row up the great river to its very head waters, high in the Canadian Rockies. The river journey would be long and hard—and that was only the beginning.

Alexander Ross had decided to make the trip with Simpson to help interpret for Garry. To replace Ross, one of the other Hudson's Bay Company men stayed behind to help manage Spokane House. But no one in the expedition could speak the Kootenai tongue.

Once the boats had drifted out of sight around the bend in the river, a large crowd of Indians gathered beside the river. Garry carried only a blanket and an extra pair of moccasins. His knife and a tomahawk hung from his belt. He noticed that the other boy—who he'd learned was called Pelly—had a bow and a quiver of arrows.

Garry eyed Governor Simpson's rifle with its long blue barrel and intricately carved stock and wished that he had a fire stick like it. That would be far better than any set of bow and arrows.

Finally the time for departing had come. Chief Illim stepped forward and spoke loudly and fervently to Governor Simpson and Alexander Ross. "You see, we have given you our sons—not our servants or our slaves, but our own children. We have given you our hearts—but bring them back again before they become white men. We wish to see them again as one of our own people. Do not let them get sick or die. If they get sick, we get sick; if they die, we, too, shall die. Take them; they are yours."

Governor Simpson nodded and stepped forward. With equal solemnity, he reached out and shook the hand of the chief. "I will do as you ask."

Then he turned to Garry and Pelly, who were standing side by side at this point. Looking at each of them in turn, he asked a question that Ross quickly interpreted for Garry and then Chief Illim interpreted for Pelly: "We are glad you boys are making this journey to the Red River Mission where you will learn about God so that you can bring the message back to your people. Are you willing?"

Both Garry and Pelly nodded their heads, though Garry's stomach felt as nervous as a chipmunk at the thought of traveling so far. He glanced at Pelly, who looked terrified. But what else could they do? Their fathers were sending them to the mission.

"Then," said Simpson through his interpreters, "I give you these blankets in solemn pledge to do my best to care for you on this journey." He handed them each a new red blanket.

At this, the women from the two tribes began to moan and cry softly, but Chief Illim raised his hand. "Do not weaken them with your wailing. They are men, being sent out on a man's quest. Make their hearts brave as you would if they were going on a buffalo hunt." Then he stepped forward and grasped the right hand of each boy and put it in the hand of Alexander Ross. The women stopped crying, and the chief said, "It is your task, our sons, to bring back to us the Leaves of Life. Do not fail us! Do not fail the old prophecy!"

Then he turned and walked away, and all the villagers followed him without looking back at the boys as the expedition mounted their horses and headed down the trail that wound its way along the Spokane River. Garry's brother, Sultz-lee, would accompany them as far as the Columbia River in order to return the horses to the village.

Garry, too, did not look back. Nor did he trust himself to say good-bye. All he could think about in that moment was that it would be many years before he saw his father again.

Chapter 5

The Expedition

The mounted brigade of fur traders had no sooner passed Eagle Rock on the shortcut that cut off one of the first large loops of the Spokane River than it began to rain. The white men turned up the collars on their black wool coats and pulled their wide-brimmed hats low over their eyes. Garry rode on until he was shivering from the cold spring rain. Finally he unrolled his new red Hudson's Bay Company blanket and wrapped it around him, pulling it up over his head, leaving only a narrow tunnel to look through over the ears of his paint.

Pelly, who was riding in front of him, turned around and saw that

Garry had gotten out his blanket, so he did the same.

Then the chilling rain turned to hail. The stones were no larger than rabbit droppings at first and merely stung Garry's exposed hands that held the reins. He tried to pull the blanket over them, but the wind shifted around to the west, driving the hail right through the opening in his blanket. Soon the hailstones grew to the size of a bird's egg. They hurt, even through the blanket.

Up ahead, Garry heard a horse whinny and Governor Simpson cry out in angry protest. In spite of the hail, Garry let the blanket slip back so he could see. Simpson's horse had spooked, perhaps from the hail striking it so hard. The animal reared while Simpson clung to its back. Then the animal began to buck while Simpson slowly began to slide to one side in his saddle until he could not keep from falling off. The governor rolled as he hit the ground, luckily avoiding the pounding hooves of his mount.

Relieved of its rider, the horse galloped on up the trail with the stirrups of the white man's saddle flapping like the wings of a goose, nearly igniting other horses it passed into a similar panic.

Garry let his blanket fall to the ground, reined his horse out of line, and urged it into a full gallop up through the woods far enough away from the trail so as not to frighten the other horses. When he came back onto the path, he was in full pursuit of Simpson's runaway. In just a few minutes, he drew alongside, grabbed the reins, and pulled both horses to a trot before he turned around. The runaway's eyes were still wide, showing a rim of white, its ears laid back, and it snorted again and again, trying to pull the reins free as they approached the expedition, but Garry kept it firmly under control until he delivered it to the governor, who had regained his feet.

As Simpson tried to brush the mud off his pants, he said something to Ross—Garry caught the word "Thanks"—who turned to Garry. "Governor Simpson wants to thank you for your quick thinking, Garry. Otherwise, he might have lost his mount."

By then, the hail had melted into a steady, bone-chilling drizzle that continued for the remainder of the day and on into the night, when it finally ended and the clouds began to break, allowing the moon to peek through.

Mr. Ross rode his horse alongside Garry. "Garry, I wonder if you would take the lead now that it is dark. I think your pony may be the most surefooted, and besides, you are probably more familiar with this country than any of the rest of us."

Garry kicked his paint to the front of the column without comment. He had traveled the forty-five miles down the Spokane River to the mighty Columbia with his father several times, but he had never come this far on this trail. Still, he had no doubt that his little paint could find his way, even when the clouds obscured the moon.

It was well past midnight before they arrived at the Columbia. For some reason the men with the boats had put ashore on the other side of the Spokane, but the fire they had going on the beach certainly looked inviting. Soon they pushed one of the boats out into the water and came over to get the riders.

Governor Simpson and Mr. Ross stripped their saddles off their horses while Sultz-lee tied the horses in a line and prepared to head back to the village. Just as Garry was ready to get into the white man's boat, his brother came up to him and grabbed him in a hard hug. With unshed tears catching the glint of the moon, he slapped Garry on the back one last time and then turned away to head back up the trail.

The slightest glow was emerging along the eastern horizon when Governor Simpson roused the company from their resting places around the fire and said, "It's time to get on the river. We've got many days ahead of us!"

Nevertheless, before the stars winked out in the lightening sky, the creak of the oars and steady splash of the boat's bow into the waves of the great river had lulled Garry back to sleep on the pile of supplies in the bottom of the boat.

He awoke with the glare of spring sunshine in his eyes, so white it made him squint, but it didn't provide much warmth. He sat up, and it took him several moments before he figured out where he was.

He had never traveled up the Columbia River, but to the east he recognized the peaks of the Huckleberry Range—Spokane Mountain, Bear Mountain, Deer Mountain, and Blue Mountain. He had viewed each of them from the other side when hunting on Twin Mountains not far from his village.

He looked north, up the valley down which the Columbia flowed, and felt panic churning in his stomach like salmon trying to jump up the rapids. Soon he would be out of the territory where he could recognize anything, not the mountains or the rivers or familiar trees like Lone Pine. He would soon be a stranger in a strange land. He started looking around for landmarks so he could find his way home—a large meadow by the river, a snow-capped peak to the west, a towering rock formation that looked a little like a horse's head hanging out over the water . . . but would he recognize it coming downstream? They were passing an island with a large pile of snags caught on the upstream edge. But that could all wash away with a heavy spring rain.

Garry could not remember ever being lost. As a child, the Spokane River and the mountains around their village always gave him landmarks that were easy to locate. Even as he got older and went with the women of the village to gather camas roots or pick chokecherries, it was only into the next valley or over a familiar hill—easy to remember and find his way home. And later when he went hunting and fishing with the men, it was the same, adding one or two new mountains or streams each trip to territory he already knew.

But now everything was new, and as the morning passed, he began to fear that he wouldn't be able to find his way back. Loneliness overwhelmed him, as though drowning in deep water with no bottom.

The white man at the oars in front of him, who

actually faced the back of the boat so he could pull on the oars, pointed to a leather bag in the bottom of the boat and muttered some instruction. Garry recognized the words "food" and "eat." He opened the bag and found some kind of a biscuit and rancid-smelling jerky. The man indicated that he could have some, so Garry dug out a piece of each and handed the bag to the man, who took his share before passing it to the other men.

Garry began gnawing on the jerky and then noticed the oarsman banging his biscuit on the edge of the boat, knocking out some bugs before taking a bite. Garry did the same, but when he tried to bite into it, the biscuit was nearly as hard as a piece of wood. He had to gnaw at it like a beaver for several minutes before getting a bite.

The oarsman grinned at him and then in a mixture of words and signs asked if he wanted to take his place at the oar. Garry agreed, thinking he ought to do his part.

The two wooden boats traveled continually from before dawn to well after dark. All the men took turns rowing—even Governor Simpson took a turn. At night, everyone was so exhausted that they did little more than build a fire and make coffee before everyone had fallen asleep, sometimes right on the sand.

Occasionally the rapids of the river were so rough that they had to pull into the shallows and get out and wade upstream, pulling the boats along behind them with ropes. This was always agonizing work.

The water was so cold that at first Garry's feet throbbed with such pain it was as though he had dropped boulders on them. Soon, however, the pain would mercifully subside as he lost all feeling in his feet and legs, but then it was nearly impossible to find his footing as they struggled forward. Again and again, first one and then another of the travelers fell to his knees, bruising or cutting them on the sharp stones. This sudden shift of weight on the towrope would often cause another person to lose his balance, and sometimes they would all end up facedown in the water before they could regain control against the swift current.

In two weeks, however, the party had traveled 340 miles north to the headwaters of the Columbia River and Kinbasket Lake, deep in the Canadian Rockies. Garry had finally conquered his fear of not knowing where he was. The river and the mountain ranges themselves seemed more recognizable as he traveled along with them each day. And even though he had never been in this part of the north country, he could imagine getting home from where he was . . . if he could build a canoe strong enough to survive some of the rough water of the river.

Garry looked at his hands. His palms were covered with bloody, oozing sores where blisters from rowing had formed, broken, torn off, and then new ones had formed again. He could hardly close his hands, let alone think about building a canoe.

But when he realized that they had pulled their boats up onto a beach at the approach to Athabasca Pass for the final time, he jumped out and fell down on his stomach, kissing the ground. The men near him laughed, and a couple of them did the same, but Pelly just stood watching with a haunted look in his eyes.

Governor Simpson lost no daylight celebrating, however. Each person was outfitted with a pack of the remaining supplies, and they headed up the trail into the mountains. These were mountains like none Garry had ever seen. They soared up into the clouds in great sweeps of treeless granite or fields of crumbling shale, and in many of the valleys between the peaks Garry saw glaciers.

In fact, the next morning, only an hour after they had set out on the trail, it began to snow. The snow fell like the water over Nine Mile Falls, piling up so quickly that it was hard to detect the trail. Finally, when it was two feet deep and clinging to their frozen legs with every step, the clouds began to part and the snow stopped. The mountain was blanketed in silence broken only by the panting of the travelers as they plodded through the snow's depths.

Soon Garry began to hear big sniffs and finally a muffled whimper. He turned and looked back at Pelly, but the other Indian boy had his blanket up over his head, leaving his face unseen. The whimpers became louder, and when Garry looked back, it was obvious that Pelly was staggering. Garry realized that he was crying so hard he couldn't keep his balance.

He stepped aside to walk beside Pelly, though it meant he had to break his own trail, making the going much harder. Even though he couldn't speak Pelly's language, he put his hand on the boy's shoulder. Pelly drew back with a start, letting the blanket fall from his head even though it revealed his tear-stained face.

Garry patted him on the shoulder, and then, noticing a robin huddled under an outcropping of rock beside the trail, he pointed the bird out to Pelly and grinned. Robins had barely returned to the Spokane before they had left. What was one doing this far north and this high so early in the spring?

Pelly sniffed hard, but the beginning of a *wow-that's-something* grin tugged at the edge of his mouth. Even without words, Garry and Pelly looked at each other with new understanding. They were brothers here, a long way from home, and they needed to stick together. With Garry's encouragement, the younger boy fell back into line behind him as the expedition wound its way up the snow-bound trail.

Chapter 6

Diving for the Fire Stick

Coming down into a sweeping valley on the far side of the high pass, the brigade spotted a welcome sight—smoke drifting lazily from the stone chimney of a trading post hugging the shores of Brule Lake, which was just an exceptionally wide and calm section of the Athabasca River. Unlike the white man's squat log house on the Spokane River, Jasper House, as this trading post was called, was made of sawed planks. There was a second story, several windows, and a porch that ran the whole length of the structure.

Garry was curious. He had seen Mr. Ross cut boards from logs at Spokane House. Ross often hired local Indians to do the work, with one man down in a pit operating one end of a saw and another above pulling back and forth on the other end. But it took days to cut up one log. And here was a whole building built of these planks.

That night as they bedded down with their blankets in one of the upstairs rooms, Pelly gingerly peeled off his damp moccasins. Garry winced. Pelly's feet had several angry blisters and bloody cuts from sharp trail stones. No wonder he had been crying! Garry went downstairs and got a pan of warm water and some rags to bathe and clean the other boy's feet. He was worried. No way could Pelly keep walking on those feet till they healed.

But the next morning, they saw supplies being loaded into six canoes and hurried to help. Garry and Pelly got one of the smaller canoes to themselves, Indian-built, probably traded at Jasper House for some Hudson's Bay supplies. With the sun rising into an azure sky, they dipped their paddles into the emerald waters of Brule Lake. The unusual milky-green color of the water, Mr. Ross told them, came from the minerals scoured by the glaciers that fed the Athabasca River. Along the horizon, the peaks of the Rockies looked like the teeth of the saws the white men used to cut logs.

By midafternoon they had paddled out of the end of Brule Lake and into the Athabasca River, now a clear emerald green, as some of the mineral sediment that had given the water its earlier milky appearance dropped as it passed through the slow-moving lake.

At dusk, the expedition stopped and made camp on a broad sandy beach. Governor Simpson said that even with a moon out that night, it would be too easy to lose a canoe if one struck an underwater rock in the rapids. Before the purple left the sky, Pelly motioned to Garry to follow him into the woods. Once they were out of sight of the white men, Pelly pulled his bow off his back and notched an arrow. He pointed Garry to go in one direction, while he followed a narrower trail through deeper undergrowth.

Garry had gone only a hundred yards when he came to the edge of a small meadow. He could just make out the shapes of a half dozen deer grazing. He looked back toward the river, which was now out of sight, and wondered how Pelly knew the meadow was there. Obviously Pelly wanted him to move the deer to the other side of the meadow, where he would be waiting to shoot one of them. But he had to give Pelly a few more minutes to get into position.

He was almost within range to try a shot from where he stood . . . if only he had brought his own bow and arrows! But he'd been upset at not getting to race for Governor Simpson's rifle.

Regretting his foolishness, Garry slowly dropped to his knees and crept silently toward the deer just to see if he could get closer. Another mistake. He succeeded in getting closer, but when the deer finally did notice him, they spooked and bolted across the meadow much faster than if they'd seen him at a greater distance and drifted back into the far woods. Now Pelly would have a much harder time hitting his mark.

Nevertheless, Garry heard the telltale twang of Pelly's bow followed instantly by a thump and wild thrashing through the brush instead of the graceful bounds of an escaping deer. "Did you get one?" called Garry quietly, forgetting that Pelly did not speak Spokane. But the other boy understood enough to answer with a muffled, "Yes."

The waning but almost full moon had just risen to stream its ghostly beams through the branches of the fir trees when the boys found the downed deer. Pelly quickly gutted the carcass while Garry cut a pole to make it easier to carry the meat back to camp.

Everyone was grateful for that night's feast, and the boys, whom the trappers had generally ignored before this, became welcome heroes that night. "You can do this every night," said Mr. Ross, tearing a hunk of roasted venison off a bone with his teeth.

The next morning, Garry and Pelly's canoe led the expedition down the gently curving Athabasca as mist rose from its calm surface like golden smoke in the slanting rays of the morning light. With the sun still at such a low angle, the water looked black, and Garry, who was standing in the front of the canoe, did not notice the huge shape moving below the surface until he hit it with his paddle.

A huge head erupted from the dark water—a moose with antlers large enough to serve a banquet on! The wave created by its sudden upsurge nearly tipped over the canoe, and Garry nearly lost his paddle grabbing the sides. A dripping beard of green

river grass hung from the animal's enormous mouth, but Garry shoved the tip of his paddle into the beast's nose and pushed off as hard as he could, sending the canoe skimming down the river out of the animal's reach.

But the boys' canoe wasn't the only intruder on the moose's peaceful breakfast. Five other canoes followed, and the one carrying Governor Simpson was headed right for it. The moose snorted and lunged toward the canoe, soon putting itself into deep water so that it had to swim. But its powerful hooves drove it forward before the governor and his companion could swerve out of the way. The tip of the velvet-covered antlers caught the edge of the canoe and rolled it over in an instant, throwing both men, a bale of furs, a tent, and the governor's beautiful rifle into the icy water.

"Turn around!" Garry yelled. He backstroked with his paddle, and Pelly pulled hard on his paddle to turn their canoe. But the moose wasn't through with his rampage and was heading straight for the governor. "Go! Go! Go!" yelled Garry as Pelly headed the prow of their canoe between the advancing moose head and the governor, who was struggling to keep his head above water.

It was a dangerous move, since the moose could have flipped their canoe as easily as it had the governor's. But the yelling boys, advancing with a frenzy in their canoe, confused the moose, who probably thought he had had enough trouble for one morning. Turning aside, the moose swam back to the shore just as two of the other canoes arrived on the scene.

Quickly Garry and Pelly and the other men maneuvered to rescue the governor and his companion and pick up the floating baggage. The capsized canoe was a little more difficult, as it was nearly submerged and as hard to handle as an old log. Garry grabbed one side and Alexander Ross in another canoe grabbed the other, and together the rescuers managed to pull it to the shore.

"What about your fire stick?" Garry pointed to where he'd seen it splash into the river. Ross translated for the governor.

"It's gone! Gone for good!" said Simpson, struggling out of his wet clothes to wring them out. "Someone get a fire going before we freeze to death!"

Garry ran to collect an armload of driftwood. When he dumped the wood down onto the beach, he said, "If I get it, can I have it?"

Simpson caught the gist of his words and gestures. "What? You think you can dive into that freezing water?"

Garry nodded and pounded his chest with his forefinger. "Can I have it?"

The governor waved a go-ahead but then muttered, "You better not catch your death. I promised your father I'd take good care of you."

Garry peeled off his tunic, kicked off his moccasins, and pulled Pelly toward their canoe. In just a few minutes, they were back upstream at the point where they had met the moose. Without hesitating, Garry was over the side, diving down into the chilling darkness. The water was so cold that he had to try twice before he could even reach the bottom—so full of weeds it would be almost impossible to find anything.

When he broke the surface, Garry knew he had only one more chance. The cold was sapping all his energy, and he was already beginning to shiver uncontrollably. Pelly was saying something to him and pointing out into a little deeper water. Garry turned in the direction Pelly had pointed, took a huge breath, and ducked under one more time. Down . . . down . . . down he went, unable to see a thing in the gloom. Suddenly his hand jammed into a moss-covered boulder on the bottom. His fingers were so cold that they felt like he had dropped the boulder on them rather than just stubbing his fingers.

He flipped over, feet down, when he felt something long and thin scrape along his leg. He reached down, grabbed it, and headed toward the surface. But when he broke into the welcome air and raised his hand in triumph, he discovered he had retrieved only a waterlogged stick. His hands had been so cold he couldn't tell that it wasn't the stock of the rifle. Throwing it aside, he grabbed the side of the canoe to catch his breath, ready to give up.

Only then did he realize that over the three dives, they had drifted downstream from the place where the moose had flipped the governor's canoe. "Back there," he said, pointing upstream a short distance. "Take me back."

Pelly gave a few strong strokes with his paddle, pulling Garry upstream.

"Here," Garry said, his teeth chattering so loudly that Pelly couldn't have understood what he was saying even if he knew Spokane. But that didn't matter, because Garry had ducked underwater one more time. Down he went, his arms and legs barely strong enough to pull him deeper. When he reached the bottom, he felt around among the stones until his lungs felt like they were going to rip open. Suddenly his hand touched something that moved away. He grabbed at it and grabbed again, catching something long and hard. He pulled it close to his face and in the dim light saw that he had finally found the rifle.

But as Garry pushed toward the surface, he could no longer hold his breath. Air exploded from his lungs, and he knew that he couldn't keep from sucking in, but—would it be air or water? He thought he was rising, but it was getting darker as though he were sinking. Just before blacking out, he burst from the surface.

The next thing he knew he was lying on his back on the beach staring up at lacy clouds floating through a deep blue sky. Garry coughed and sat up. The members of the expedition all stood around him, and there was Pelly, kneeling in front of him and grinning as though his face would split. In his hand, with the butt planted firmly on the sand, was the governor's rifle, still dripping from its bath in the river.

Governor Simpson was true to his word and let Garry keep the rifle. "Here," he said, pointing to the carving on the stock of the rifle, " 'Simpson.' My name." He pointed to himself, and at first Garry thought he was asking for it back. But the governor turned to Ross. "Tell him it's just my name. At the mission they'll teach him to read. Then he'll always remember where he got it." The governor also gave

Garry a powder horn and shot, and in the evenings before dark, he showed him how to load and shoot.

The rifle had so much more range than a bow and arrow, but it was still hard to hit the center of a stump at two hundred paces. At first, Garry jerked the rifle every time he pulled the trigger. Fire and black smoke exploded with a big bang so close to his face that he couldn't help but flinch. Still, with practice, he got better and couldn't wait to go hunting.

Two more days of easy travel down the Athabasca brought the travelers to flatter country with rolling hills only a couple hundred feet in height on either side of the smooth river. That afternoon as they rounded a bend in the glassy river, Garry saw smoke rising in the distance from some buildings on the bank of the river.

"There's the fort!" shouted one of the trappers as everyone dug in their paddles to cover the last remaining mile to Fort Assiniboine.

Garry and Pelly kept in the lead of the other canoes as they approached the fort until they saw a dozen or more tepees creating a village outside the picket walls of the fort. Then they slowed up to let the other men lead the way. "What tribe are they?" Garry asked Alexander Ross as he passed in his canoe.

Ross shrugged. "Several tribes. They come from all over, but they're all friendly. They just come to trade."

But when the expedition had beached their canoes and walked stiffly through the little village of tepees to the gates of the huge fort, Garry saw the strange Indians and some of the white trappers lounging near the gate eyeing his new rifle as though they didn't think he should have such a fine weapon.

That night, the boys were directed to a hay barn to sleep. With the winter past, it was nearly empty, but there was still enough hay to make comfortable beds for the weary travelers. Garry lay down, pulling his Hudson's Bay blanket over him, and fell instantly asleep, one arm over the rifle that lay beside him like a favorite walking stick.

He slept so soundly that he did not notice when a tall dark shape bent over him, lifted his arm, and drew out the rifle.

Chapter 7

Thunder Dragons

As soon as Garry awoke, he knew something was wrong, but it took him a moment to realize what it was.

"My rifle! Pelly, where's my rifle! Pelly!" He shook his companion awake and yanked him to a sitting position. "Where's my rifle?" he yelled.

He motioned wildly with his hands, making up signs, but Pelly had understood the words and was already looking around, bewildered. He began digging in the hay as though he was sure it had to be nearby.

Garry stood up, stomped to the barn door and back, waving his arms and yelling. "Someone stole my rifle. Somebody stole it! Somebody stole it! I'm going to find out who the thief is and take it back!"

"Simpson? Governor Simpson?" Pelly shrugged.

"What?" He stopped pacing. "Governor Simpson? You think he took it back?"

Pelly shrugged again.

Garry went back to the barn door, opened it a crack, and peered out. The fort was coming to life for the day; men drifted past carrying armloads of wood and buckets of water. He looked back at Pelly. "You think Governor Simpson took it back?"

Pelly held his hands out, palms up, shrugged, and raised his eyebrows in a *who-knows?* expression.

Garry opened the barn door and went out, intent on confronting the governor.

"Ah, Spokane Garry," said Alexander Ross when he saw Garry coming. "You look raring to go. Glad to see you up so early. We need to make an early start today."

Ross's jovial manner took some of the steam out of Garry. "Uh, Mr. Ross, does the Governor have a rifle?"

"Did he get a rifle? Oh yeah, and he better hang on to it this time! Now, go get Pelly and meet us behind the trading post. There'll be coffee and something to eat. We're going by horse for the next ninety miles, all the way to Fort Edmonton. Now get!"

Garry turned and walked slowly back to the barn, head down, letting his feet drag in the dust. Why would the governor do that? Why would he give him his rifle only to take it back? It didn't make sense!

The governor was supposed to know about God, and Garry had already learned that God did not approve of stealing. To Garry, this was the same as stealing.

On the other hand, the rifle did have the governor's name on it in those strange markings white men made. Maybe that meant it would always belong to him and he had only allowed Garry to carry and shoot it for a short while.

When the expedition gathered for departure, Garry watched the governor mount up. Sure enough, the governor tied a long, leather scabbard to his saddle—the kind that held a rifle. He could see it from across the yard; no need to go ask the governor. With head hanging, Garry swung up on the mount that had been assigned to him. It was a bony nag that his Spokane people would have used for bear bait, but none of the other horses were very enviable, either. Garry fell in line near the rear of the column that headed out of the fort. As he rode along, he wondered whether anyone would notice if he ducked into the woods and headed south. If he had a better horse, he might even try it. After all, what could these white men teach their people about God if they didn't even keep their word?

But that evening, when the column of travelers stopped for camp by a small stream, Governor Simpson called Garry over to him. "Son, see if you can shoot us a deer in that meadow downstream."

Garry just stared at him. What an unthinkable request after taking back his gun!

"Well, go on! We could use some fresh meat after such a long ride."

All right. If that's how the governor wanted it. Clenching his teeth, Garry walked over to the governor's horse and reached for the rifle.

"Hey, use your own rifle!" said the governor.

Putting his hands on his hips, Garry turned in appeal to Mr. Ross, who was standing nearby. What was this, some kind of a joke or test? "I don't have it," he said tersely.

"What do you mean, you don't have it?" asked Ross.

Garry pointed toward the governor's horse. "The governor took it back."

"What? You think that's your gun? What makes you think he'd take it? The governor bought a different rifle back at the fort. Where's the one he gave you?"

Confused, Garry turned and looked more carefully at the gun in the scabbard on the governor's horse. The carving on the stock . . . it . . . it was completely different, without the letters that spelled Simpson! This *was* a different rifle! "I . . . I don't know," he stammered, turning back to Ross. "This morning it was gone. I . . . I thought Governor Simpson took it back. I didn't know—"

"You telling us someone stole your rifle back at the fort?" Ross turned to Simpson and quickly explained in English what Garry had told him.

"What?" said Simpson. "Who?"

Garry shrugged and explained how he had slept with the rifle right by his side but in the morning it was gone. "Pelly even helped me look for it."

"Do you have any idea who else might have taken it?" asked Ross.

Garry was going to say no but then recalled how several Indians and trappers had stared at him when he entered the fort. "Maybe one of them snuck into the barn and—"

"I'll write a letter when we get to Fort Edmonton," said Ross, "and send it with the next travelers west. Maybe someone at Fort Assiniboine will come across it. But don't get your hopes up. A lost rifle could be as hard to retrieve as gossip."

They had no fresh venison that night. Garry went to bed under the stars telling himself he ought to feel better knowing that Governor Simpson hadn't lied to him or taken his rifle. But the fact that he might never get back such a prized possession left him feeling like flint without steel.

The expedition covered the ninety miles from Fort Assiniboine to Fort Edmonton in two days, but once in Edmonton, they had to wait while fourteen flat-bottomed cargo boats were prepared to travel down the Saskatchewan River. Some were still being built. In addition to the furs the governor's expedition had with them, other trappers had sent their bales of furs to Edmonton for sale and shipment.

Garry welcomed the rest from the hard travel, but he found the fort a bewildering marvel of the white man's world. Situated on an eroding bluff above the river, it was as ugly a place to build a village as any place Garry could imagine. "Like an old scab on a bald man's head," he muttered to Mr. Ross.

"Yes," laughed Mr. Ross, "but it is easy to defend. No one can get within a mile without being seen." From the wall of the fort high above the river, Garry thought the boats looked like a swarm of bees moving around on the water below.

Garry and Pelly spent the two-week layover at Fort Edmonton listening to and trying out as much English as they could learn. Garry had learned a little from the traders back at Spokane House, but after spending several weeks with English-speaking people, both boys had picked up quite a lot. Quick to learn, they pitched in to help finish the boats, then helped with the loading of supplies and bundles of winter furs.

On the day of their departure, the Simpson party was down at the riverfront early, finding their places in the boats and getting ready to push off when Garry noticed a trapper on a horse pulling two pack mules that were skidding down the trail to the water's edge. "Hold on! Hold on!" the man hollered. Mr. Ross clambered off the boat to speak to the man. In a few moments he was back.

"Says he just arrived from Fort Assiniboine, hoping to catch our flotilla of boats before it left."

"We're ready to go," Governor Simpson yelled to the man. "We can't take time to load any more furs. You'll have to wait for the next shipment."

"But I can't wait!" the trapper protested, dismounting from his lathered horse.

"What do you mean, you can't wait?" said Simpson. "They'll pay you the same for your furs up in the fort."

"It's not just my furs. It's me! *I've* got to go with you. Uh—my sister's sick back East, and I've gotta get back to see her . . . 'fore she dies."

The governor frowned and looked around at the boats, as though considering whether he had space for the trapper. As Simpson and Ross conferred, Garry stared hard at the bearded trapper. He'd seen this man before . . . back at Fort Assiniboine.

Scrambling over the side of the flat-bottom boat still beached below the cliff, Garry circled behind the man and casually examined the packs on the mules. On the far side of the second mule, the edge of a rifle butt stuck out from beneath some furs. Reaching beneath the furs, he pulled on the rifle butt just enough till he could see the English letters carved into the wood: SIMPSON.

An iron hand clamped on his wrist. "Hey! What you think you doin'?" snarled the trapper's voice in his ear.

"He's got the rifle!" Garry yelled in Spokane. "The governor's rifle!"

Mr. Ross came running.

"What's he sayin'?" growled the man. "He's a thievin' Indian, that's what."

"Where'd you get that rifle?" Mr. Ross demanded. The man narrowed his eyes, wary as a cornered

wildcat. Then he cracked a wide grin and pulled out the rifle from the mule pack. "This here rifle? Why, I traded three beaver pelts for it back at Fort Assiniboine."

By this time the governor was off the boat and had joined them. "That gun was stolen from us back at Fort Assiniboine." He reached out for the rifle.

"Ah!" said the trapper, pulling back as swiftly as a cat. "If it's this here gun you want, it comes with me and my furs."

"Let me see it first," the governor demanded. Reluctantly the trapper handed it over. The governor examined it a moment. Without doubt it was the stolen rifle.

"Well, now, I can't help it if somebody stole that rifle, then sold it to me, can I?" The trapper waggled his hairy eyebrows. "But I'm a generous man. Might just give it back—even if it did cost me three pelts—but the least you can do is return the favor and let me on one of these here boats."

"All right, all right," snapped the governor. "Find yourself a spot, but make it quick. We're supposed to be casting off right now." Simpson turned and tossed the rifle to Garry. "Keep closer tabs on this from now on."

Garry caught the rifle and climbed into the boat. He was so engrossed in looking it over that he didn't even notice when the boats pushed out into the river. It was his prize rifle, all right, and except for a scratch on the stock, it looked no worse for the wear. Maybe this trip wouldn't turn out so bad, after all, even though his father had sent him away.

But he didn't believe for a minute that the man had paid three beaver pelts for it. Bet he didn't have a sick sister, either.

Travel down the Saskatchewan River was relatively easy. They mostly floated with the current, but the nearly two hundred miles across Cedar Lake and Lake Winnipeg to Norway House, the next trading post, required constant rowing, even though they were able to put up small sails occasionally when the wind was favorable.

The expedition arrived at Norway House on June 14, with the gnats nearly as thick in the air as smoke from a pitch fire. But it wasn't the clouds of insects in the air that were the problem. It was when they bit and got in one's eyes, nose, mouth, and ears. Garry found himself spitting and slapping more than he was rowing, especially when they were anywhere near land.

After a couple days' rest at Norway House, the flotilla set out once more for the three-hundred-mile trip down Lake Winnipeg and up the Red River. Day after day they rowed, the boys' muscles growing firm and strong. As they traveled up the Red River, they began to see more and more of what Alexander Ross explained were farms where white people lived and planted grain and food in the ground and kept their cattle instead of hunting their meat and gathering the nuts and berries that grew wild. Sometimes several farmhouses were built together in a little village. People waved to them from the river's bank, and children would run down to the water's edge to watch them pass.

Garry had lost count of the days. But finally the expedition turned its boats ashore just before reaching old Fort Gibraltar. Its stockade walls were much taller and stronger than Fort Edmonton, and it was positioned more pleasantly, dominating the prairie on the west bank of the river.

Garry and Pelly helped drag their boat ashore and got out stiffly, tired from such a long trip. In seventy-five days, they had traveled 1,850 miles from the Spokane. Garry held tightly to his rifle as he stared up at the fort. It was so strange—and scary—to be this far from home.

Suddenly fire and smoke belched from what looked like the long heads of two black horses peering over the top of the walls on either side of the gate. The explosions were accompanied by a thunderous roar so loud that both boys fell to the mud, hiding between the boats.

Thunder dragons, thought Garry. *They have brought us here to feed us to thunder dragons!*

Chapter 8

Just a Little Horse Race

With the thunder still echoing down the river, Mr. Ross said, "Get up, boys," while trying to keep from laughing uproariously like the other men who were bent over and wiping tears from their eyes. "They're only firing the cannons to welcome us. Did you think we were under attack?"

"Attack?" said Garry, rising to his hands and knees while keeping a sharp eye on the black "dragons" peering over the wall of the fort. "Attack by the thunder dragons?"

"Of course not. Those are only cannons, just like your rifle, but much, much larger. What did you think they were?"

Garry eyed the black "heads" on the wall. "Thunder dragons. I thought they were thunder dragons." But just then he saw men pull whatever the black things were back from the edge and ram a stick down their throats, as though feeding the dragons . . . or was it like the ramrod he used to clean and load his rifle? "Cannon? Like my rifle?" he said, looking at Alexander Ross with narrowed eyes.

"Yes, cannons. Just big guns. Very big. Instead of firing shot the size of a chokecherry, they fire a ball as large as two fists together. They're just guns."

Garry and Pelly stood up and hung their heads, letting their long black hair swing forward, half covering their reddening faces. The men's laughter had died to small chuckles as they shook their heads and returned to unloading the boats. "Don't worry about it," said Alexander Ross. "There'll be a lot of new things to see in the next few days. Just stay calm, and . . . and ask questions."

Alexander Ross and Governor Simpson herded the boys up the riverbank and through the huge gates of the stockade into the fort. Garry looked up at the "dragons." Apparently Mr. Ross was right. What had looked like giant horses' heads from a distance were merely black tubes mounted on small wheels. So that was a cannon.

But that wasn't the only strange thing Garry saw at the bustling fort: large wooden boxes that rolled on wheels, pulled by mules; a young girl and her mother with white skin and hair the color of grass at the end of summer; and so many people.

A creeping feeling overcame Garry, similar to what he'd felt when he first learned that his father was exiling him. This place could be a "prison" from which he might never escape!

"Garry . . . Garry." Garry heard Mr. Ross calling his name as Mr. Ross stood before a man with a small beard and a wide-brimmed black hat. "This is Reverend David T. Jones. He's in charge of the Red River Mission, where you'll be going to school. It's run by the Church of England."

Garry had no idea what the Church of England was, but he reached his hand out in the fashion of white people to greet Rev. Jones with a handshake.

"Glad to have you boys," said Rev. Jones. "I just have a few more items of business to do here, and then we can be on our way to your school."

"Reverend Jones," said Governor Simpson, stepping up. He put his hand over his mouth as though saying something privately, but Garry was close enough and could now understand enough English to catch most of it. "I just want to warn you, Reverend, to take — care of these boys. They are sons of chiefs, chiefs of — influence in the Columbia —. Any accident could stir up warfare with what have been peaceful tribes. You will take care, won't you?"

Rev. Jones looked at the boys and raised his eyebrows as though really seeing them for the first time. "Certainly," he said, giving a slight bow of respect. "I'll see that they are well cared for."

82

Garry could not have been more relieved than when he walked out of the gates of the huge fort. At least he wasn't being held captive inside its high walls.

The mission school was about a mile north of the fort, back down the river from where they had beached their boats, now fully unloaded. The mission seemed like a small village, for besides the school building—as Rev. Jones explained—there was also a church, a barn, and several homes for missionaries and schoolteachers, all made of logs, not unlike Spokane House near Garry's home.

Rev. Jones guided the boys to one of these log homes where he introduced them to a teacher named Mr. Arnold Worthington. The main room of Mr. Worthington's "lodge," as Garry thought of it, was arranged at one end as a dormitory with bunk beds for six boys. At the other end was a large table built of rough-sawn planks with benches on either side. Beyond the table, the wall was dominated by a huge stone fireplace with its own smoke hole, a chimney similar to the one at Spokane House that let the smoke out before it floated through the room and made your eyes burn.

In the back wall was a doorway that led to Mr. Worthington's private quarters, but the thing that intrigued Garry most were the large square holes in the front wall on either side of the door. He walked over to inspect one, even as Mr. Worthington was explaining that the other boys were out working in the garden. But when Garry got close to the hole, he could see that it was filled with something that he could see right through as though it were clear ice. Except for some cross sticks and wavy lines in the "ice," it was as though it wasn't there. He touched it gently. It was cold, as cold as outside, but not nearly as cold as ice, and it wasn't melting.

Spokane House had had a window but not with "ice" in it. The hole in the wall there was covered with a very thin skin greased with bear grease to let the light through. But it had not let in nearly so much light as this window.

"That's glass," said Mr. Worthington, noticing Garry's interest. "Don't hit it, or it will break."

Garry backed away, still staring through the window, moving his head from side to side and up and down, amazed that it was almost like being outside.

"Now if you boys will help me move these bunks," said Mr. Worthington, "we can make room for a bunk for you boys. I think there is an extra one in the barn."

Pelly waved his hands from side to side. "Sleep on floor. Good blanket." He held up his new Hudson's Bay blanket that was now rather dusty from the hard use on the trip.

"Oh, no, not on the floor. You boys will need a bunk like everyone else. Come on. Help me move this."

What more could they say? *Everything* might be different here in the white man's world.

Class began for Pelly and Garry the next morning. A total of sixteen Indian boys gathered in the schoolhouse, which had four large windows on each side that, to Garry's amazement, made it nearly as bright as outside. He wasn't familiar with any of the tribes from which the other students came, so English became the only common language for communicating, and, of course, it was the language of the white teachers.

When Mr. Worthington began the morning with prayer, Garry began to believe that he might learn something about God that he could take home to his people. And then Mr. Worthington opened a black book and began reading about God. Was it the "Leaves of Life" his people had so eagerly awaited? Garry hardly heard anything else the teacher said that morning—and didn't understand what he was talking about when he did try to listen.

In the middle of the day, everyone was excused from school to get something to eat before going to work on the farm, where the boys were being taught to plant crops and raise animals for food. "It's the way the white man lives," Mr. Worthington had explained. "Some day there will not be room in the land for everyone to get all they need by hunting and fishing and gathering roots and berries. So you will need to learn to farm."

Garry didn't mind the idea of learning a new way to make a living—wasn't that part of Circling Raven's prophecy?—but it sounded crazy to say that someday there wouldn't be enough land.

When the other boys left, Garry hung back and eased his way to the front of the room. The black book was on the corner of Mr. Worthington's table with some papers resting on top of it.

"Yes, Garry?" said Mr. Worthington, glancing up briefly from something he was writing. "Is there something I can do for you? Could you understand what we were doing this morning?"

"Hmm. School okay."

But when Garry remained standing there, Mr. Worthington finally looked up. "Well, what is it?"

"Is that the 'Leaves of Life'?"

"Bible . . . God's Holy Word." The teacher moved the papers out of the way and pointed to the marks on the cover. "See, H-o-l-y B-i-b-l-e, Holy Bible! Here, do you want to look at it?" He handed the precious book to Garry and then went back to writing. A few moments later he stopped and looked up at Garry, who was carefully holding the book as though it might break. "Go ahead, you can open it. It won't be long before you can actually read it. But"—and he raised his left hand to stroke his small beard—"what was that you called it?"

"The Leaves of Life. I think this must be the Leaves of Life. My people have been waiting for it for years."

"Waiting? What do you mean?"

Struggling for words in English, Garry told the white man about the old prophecies. While he was talking, excitement bubbled up in his chest. Maybe . . . maybe his father really *had* sent him to the Red River Mission on a quest rather than just into exile as a punishment.

By the end of summer, Garry's English was good enough that he could carry on a conversation with relative ease. He knew his alphabet and could do simple arithmetic. The Bible and The Book of Common Prayer were the only texts used in the classroom because the object was to learn the Christian faith. However, sometimes Mr. Worthington read stories to them from other books and tried to tell them about the white man's world far to the east and across the Great Sea in Europe. "Someday you might even travel there yourselves," he said.

Farming was hard work, but Garry enjoyed taking care of the animals, especially the horses, which included the horses for the Hudson's Bay Company men who lived in the fort. But what Garry couldn't understand was why white people so seldom took time to have fun. Except for the drinking that many of the trappers did when they were at the fort, it seemed as though work, work, work was all they did.

"How about a little horse race?" Garry said to Pelly and some of the other boys one beautiful September afternoon as they were cleaning out the barn. None of the boys had their own horse at the mission, but there was no rule against them riding the horses that they cared for. In fact, they often hopped on a horse to ride up to the fort on some errand or to deliver the mounts the Hudson's Bay men needed to take a short trip somewhere. So it was not long before six of the boys were sitting bareback on the best horses and ready to race down the road beside the river while several other boys looked on and made bets as to who would win.

"We race all the way to the Chief Peguis Trail and back. Agreed?" said Garry, sitting astride Governor Simpson's prancing black horse that he kept at the mission farm. "The first one back to this point wins!"

"Wait," said one of the other boys. "Do we have to stay on the road?"

"Just make it to the trail," said Garry. "Hiyeeh!" he shouted, and they were off.

All six horses galloped down the road in a pack, turning this way and that as the road hugged the bends in the river. But by the time they approached Chief Peguis Trail, the pack had begun to lengthen, and though Garry and Pelly were running neck and neck, another horse and rider were two lengths ahead.

They skidded to a stop and turned as they crossed the trail, and drove back toward the mission. Garry pulled ahead of Pelly's horse, but he could not urge enough speed out of the governor's horse to gain on the leader. Would the other horse tire? As Garry watched its long, smooth stride eat up the ground, he doubted it. It was a fine buckskin belonging to the quartermaster in the fort.

When the road began to veer left, following a bend in the river, Garry took off across the open

field. He would have to dodge occasional willow thickets and ford a small stream, but the shortcut might give him the edge.

The governor's horse leaped over the old trunk of a downed poplar tree with ease. Garry turned it left along the creek bed, galloping hard, looking for a good place to cross. He jumped the horse over a small pile of sticks, and suddenly the horse squealed as it went down, throwing Garry over its head to land on his back in the creek below.

He came up sputtering and turned quickly to make sure his mount did not get away . . . only the horse was still struggling on the bank to regain its feet. Something was wrong. Garry splashed to shore and climbed the bank, only to discover that the horse had stepped into a muskrat hole. He grabbed the reins to help pull the horse to its feet. But every time it lunged, its right leg gave way, and the horse whinnied in pain.

"Easy, easy, boy. Come on. Come on!" He tugged on the reins as the steaming animal balanced on its left front leg and then lunged to get its hindquarters under it.

Garry looked toward the road and groaned. He was not going to win this race, not with the governor's prize horse stumbling on a badly broken leg!

Chapter 9

The Ear Bite

The shot that put down Governor Simpson's horse echoed along the river, momentarily silencing the drone of the mosquitoes as the sun came to rest on the western horizon like a shimmering egg yolk.

"Now," yelled the governor, turning on Garry, "whatever possessed you to race these horses?" Without waiting for an answer, he turned to Rev. Jones. "I want this boy punished. He comes from a people that know horses, and he should have known better than to run a horse right along a creek bank or any-  where else where there might have been holes. He was just asking to break a leg. It's a wonder he didn't kill himself!"

"And what about the other boys?"

"That's your decision, Reverend, but this boy"—
he stabbed his finger in Garry's direction—"he should
have known better. That was my best horse!" He
stomped away toward the road and the buckboard
that would carry the men back toward the fort.

Mr. Worthington, however, did not hop on the
bed of the buckboard. He silently started walking up
the road after the wagon of men. The students, each
of them leading a horse except Garry, followed along
in silence.

"They just going to leave the horse carcass for
wolf bait?" Pelly finally whispered to Garry.

Garry shrugged. What difference did it make?
The horse was dead, and the governor was right. He
should have known better than to be galloping along
that creek bank. The pile of sticks he had jumped
over just before the horse had gone down had been a
muskrat lodge. It was obvious to anyone paying attention! Tunnels and holes were bound to be nearby.
He had just been too determined to win the race.

Back at the school, Rev. Jones had all the boys
gather outside the barn in the fading light, even
those who had not taken part in the race. Corporal
discipline was a public matter at the school, intended to instruct everyone about what was right
and wrong more than to humiliate the wrongdoer.
However, in the few whippings Garry had seen
since being at the school, the attention of the other
boys was far more on how brave the guilty one was

than on what he had done.

Garry pressed his lips in a thin line, determined that he wouldn't cry out.

"Mr. Worthington," instructed Rev. Jones as the boys gathered in a circle around Garry, "since he's your boy, you'll assist on this one. Assume the position, Garry."

Garry approached his teacher warily. Mr. Worthington knelt down on one knee, his back to Garry, and Garry leaned over his shoulder, allowing his teacher to grasp his hands to keep him in position. The old strap whistled through the air as Rev. Jones swung it with all his might, and then it landed with a loud smack across Garry's backside.

Garry jerked involuntarily from the pain, but Mr. Worthington held him firmly.

The strap sailed again and again, landing each time so squarely that Garry feared he would not be able to hold back a cry. In desperation, he bit his lip to keep his mouth shut. He was a Spokane, as brave as any man, and the dim evening light would mask his tears if only he could keep from crying out.

He bit down harder—one, two, three more times—and then the whipping was over. Peeling himself off Mr. Worthington's back, he stood up as straight as he could and looked around at his witnesses. Their images swam from the tears in his eyes, and the lamps shining from the windows of the buildings twinkled. In his mouth he tasted the salty thickness of blood. But like a true Spokane brave, he had uttered not one cry!

Back in his dormitory, Garry went straight to his bunk and flopped down on his stomach—his backside still stinging—and faced toward the wall. The other boys were doing their chores to prepare for supper, and Garry expected any minute for Mr. Worthington to remind him to start the fire, his task for the month. Then he heard the flames beginning to crackle in the large stone fireplace. He turned to see that Pelly had not only done his own job of bringing in the wood but had also built the fire. What a friend to cover for him so he wouldn't have to interact with the other boys until there was no chance of revealing a lingering hitch in his voice or tearstains on his cheeks.

Garry sat up and checked his lower lip with his tongue. It would not do to sport a fat lip before the other boys. But he couldn't find any cuts or sore spots. Funny, where had the blood in his mouth come from if not from his lip that he had bit to keep from crying out? He wiped his face again and breathed deeply, ready at last to face the other students.

Then he noticed Mr. Worthington standing in the corner of the room, holding a white rag to the side of his head. He pulled it away and looked at it. He put it back, but as he did so, Garry noticed that it had a bright red blotch in the center. Garry watched more closely, and every few moments, Mr. Worthington removed the rag to reveal the bright red mark. His ear was bleeding. How could that be?

By the time the boys sat down at the table for their evening's meal of corn cakes and bacon, the bleeding from Mr. Worthington's ear had ceased, apparently without anyone else noticing it. Garry kept glancing at his teacher until the man turned at one point so that the light from the table lamp shown clearly on the side of his head. There, in a hideous crescent on his ear, were red teeth marks.

The horror of what he was seeing trickled down Garry's back like melting snow: He had not bitten his own lip during the whipping. Somehow, he had bitten Mr. Worthington's *ear!*

And yet Mr. Worthington had not said a word . . . at least not yet!

"So what were you racing for so furiously this afternoon?" their teacher asked as he reached for the plate of corn cakes.

No one answered.

"Surely you had some major bet on, or you wouldn't have been running those horses so hard." He looked around the table. "Garry, you seemed to be the organizer; what would you have won if you had come in first?"

Garry swallowed. "Nothing, sir."

"Come now, you mean to tell me you were just racing for the fun of it?"

"Yes, sir." He stopped, unsure of whether to keep quiet or be more sociable. "I guess we were . . . well, the white man doesn't seem to have much fun, so we made our own fun."

"Trouble is more like it!" snorted the teacher

around a mouthful of bacon. "So you organized a race because you were bored? Is that it?" Everyone around the table slowly nodded their heads. Was Mr. Worthington going to pile more work on them? But all he did was growl, "Well, next time, try a foot race; then the only leg you'll break will be your own."

The little moon-shaped scab on Mr. Worthington's ear quickly healed, and as the months went by without anything being said about it, Garry slowly relaxed. It began to dawn on him that Mr. Worthington was not holding the injury against him, and it forged a kind of brotherhood between the two—teacher and student. Garry listened more closely in class and worked extra hard to do well in his lessons.

One morning the next spring, Mr. Worthington began class by reading from Romans 1, beginning with verse 19:

> Because that which may be known of God is manifest in [the heavens]; for God hath shewed it unto them. For the invisible things of him from the creation of the world are clearly seen, being understood by the things that are made, even his eternal power and Godhead; so that they are without excuse: Because that, when they knew God, they glorified him not as God, neither were thankful.

He read on about
how wicked people had
exchanged the glory of the immortal God for idols
they had made with their hands, idols that looked
like animals and birds and other created things,

rather than worshiping the Creator.

Garry raised his hand. "But what if those people *had* worshiped the Creator God? What if they *were* thankful? What would God have done to them?"

"Well, I'm not exactly sure, Garry. But I think God would have spoken to them in some way. God is a just God. And the Bible tells us that He is 'not willing that any should perish, but that all should come to repentance.' But why do you ask?"

Garry looked around at the other students. "Because my people have always worshiped the Creator God. We honor His creation because in doing so we honor Him, but we only *worship* the Creator."

"Well, then," said Mr. Worthington, "perhaps that is why you are here."

He closed the Bible and seemed ready to move on to some other subject, but Garry interrupted. "Not perhaps, Mr. Worthington. That's *exactly* why I am here." Why hadn't he seen it clearly before? The bubble of excitement Garry had felt at first seeing the Leaves of Life gave him courage to keep on speaking. "A prophet among our people—Circling Raven—said that white men would come, and we should learn from the Leaves of Life. The marks in them would show us how to go to heaven. I think he was talking about the black book." He pointed at Mr. Worthington's Bible. "My father sent me here to learn everything God says in the black book. It's not just perhaps. That is . . . that *is* why I am here!" When he stopped speaking, he was shaking with excitement.

"I think you may be right," said Mr. Worthington,

looking closely at the book he held in his hand. "This passage speaks of God's displeasure at those who ignore His revelation in nature, but it raises the obvious question: What if some people worship God 'in spirit and in truth'? The Gospel of John says that 'the Father seeketh such to worship him.' "

The rest of that school day, Mr. Worthington quizzed Garry about the old prophecy, asking how the Spokane people worshiped and what they had been able to understand about God just by paying attention to His revelation in nature.

"Your story is amazing," said the teacher, genuinely moved. "Here. I want to read another passage to you that talks about this subject. In Psalm 19:

The heavens declare the glory of God;
    and the firmament sheweth his handywork.
Day unto day uttereth speech,
    and night unto night sheweth knowledge.
There is no speech nor language,
    where their voice is not heard.
Their line is gone out through all the earth,
    and their words to the end of the world.

Mr. Worthington turned to the rest of the boys. "Students, do you see what this psalm is saying? The heavens—or all of nature, actually—tell us a great deal about God. But more importantly, there is no place in the whole world—'no speech nor language'— where that message is not heard. That's what Garry has told us, as well; maybe that has been true for some of you who came from other tribes.

"But that is just the beginning. There is so much more. And that is why you are here—to learn the rest of the story, the really good news. Listen what it says beginning in verse 7:

> The law of the Lord is perfect,
>   converting the soul:
> the testimony of the Lord is sure,
>   making wise the simple.
> The statutes of the Lord are right,
>   rejoicing the heart:
> the commandment of the Lord is pure,
>   enlightening the eyes.
> The fear of the Lord is clean,
>   enduring for ever:
> the judgments of the Lord are true
>   and righteous altogether.
> More to be desired are they than gold,
>   yea, than much fine gold:
> sweeter also than honey
>   and the honeycomb.
> Moreover by them is thy servant warned:
>   and in keeping of them there is great
>   reward.

Mr. Worthington closed the Bible with a thump and held it up. "In this book there is a great reward for you, a great gift! Tomorrow I'll tell you what that gift is. But for now, class is dismissed. Go get some lunch, and then get out there and hoe that corn!"

Chapter 10

The Great Gift

Garry was so eager for class to begin the next morning that after sweeping the floor—his morning duty for the month of May—he helped Pelly with his chore for the month—washing dishes.

When class began, Garry was surprised to see Rev. Jones sitting in the back of the room. But Mr. Worthington rapped for attention as the boys shuffled on their benches.

"We'll continue our study in Romans this morning and discover the great reward I mentioned to you yesterday." The teacher opened his Bible and read verses twelve through six-  teen of chapter two. "Here the apostle Paul tells us that those who have never heard of God's written Law will be judged by the law of conscience written on their heart, while those who *have* heard the Law will be judged by the Law. So I have this question: Garry, it sounds like your people learned all they could of God and His character from nature. Is that right?"

Garry nodded.

"And did you try to do what was right according to what you learned?"

"Yes, sir."

"But even by your own standards, did you succeed all the time? Did you ever lie? Was anyone ever cruel to others? Did you sometimes forget to thank God?"

"Well, y-yes," stammered Garry. "But we tried."

"Yes. I have no doubt that you tried. But I have also invited Reverend Jones to join us today because he grew up in the church, learning God's written Law from a very young age. Tell us, Reverend Jones, did knowing the Law keep you or others you knew who were equally aware of its requirements from ever sinning?"

Rev. Jones stood solemnly. "Like Garry here, we tried. But as I look back over my life, I often failed, and so did everyone else I knew."

Mr. Worthington nodded. "Thank you both for your honesty. What I think you both have shown is that whether judged by God's written Law or the law He writes on our hearts—our conscience—we all have sinned. And that's exactly what Paul tells us in Romans 3:23: 'For all have sinned, and come short of the glory of God.' Then later, in Romans 6:23, Paul tells us that 'the wages of sin is death; but the gift of God is eternal life through Jesus Christ our Lord.' 'Death' here means eternal separation from God." Mr. Worthington closed the Bible. "So there you have it. Whether growing up knowing God's laws in this book or without ever hearing the biblical message, we all sin, which separates us from God. But this book tells us about God's great gift. God wants to give you eternal life. Isn't that wonderful?"

The Indian boys just looked at him. No one spoke. Mr. Worthington looked around at his students with a slight, open-mouthed grin on his face. "Don't you see?" he asked, but still no one answered.

"Excuse me, Mr. Worthington"—the interruption came from Rev. Jones in the back of the room— "perhaps the boys don't understand how they are supposed to *get* this great gift. Maybe that is why they aren't responding."

"Of course, but it is right here in Romans."

"But you haven't told them yet."

"Indeed." Mr. Worthington looked a little flustered. He opened the Bible again. "Well, Paul says in Romans 3:22 that it comes by faith in Jesus Christ."

"But what does that mean, brother? You still haven't told them."

Mr. Worthington swallowed and looked out the windows as though he had been caught without the proper clothes on for some great festival and was looking for a place to run and hide.

"Hmm." Rev. Jones cleared his throat. "Might I

suggest you explain John 1:12 to the boys."

"Of course. Good idea. Thank you, Reverend. Now, students, during the last few weeks we have learned how God sent His only Son to earth to pay the penalty for our sins. You remember that?" There were several murmurs of agreement among the boys. "Well, John writes in his gospel, 'As many as received him, to them gave he power to become the sons of God, even to them that believe on his name.'" He glanced at Rev. Jones as though checking whether he was saying it in an understandable way.

Garry turned to look at the preacher in time to see him nodding patiently toward the teacher.

"The way we 'receive' Jesus begins—as John says in this verse—by *believing,* believing that Jesus is truly God's son, that He came to earth to take the penalty for our sins. It's as though . . ." Mr. Worthington cleared his throat. "Remember last summer when Garry got a whipping for breaking the leg of the governor's horse? What if I had stepped in and offered to take that whipping instead? *That's* what Jesus did for us when He died on the cross and rose again."

Garry looked down at the table in front of him. Mr. Worthington hadn't taken his whipping for him, but he had kept quiet when he bit his ear. Garry hadn't meant to bite his ear any more than he intended to sin against God, but it had happened, and Mr. Worthington had covered for him, protecting him from further punishment. Yes, Garry knew what it was like for someone else to take his blame.

"But," the teacher continued, "to 'receive' God's gift also means making Him the center of our lives so that He controls everything. It means giving ourselves completely to Him." His eyes were bright with hope. "Now do you understand?"

Garry kept his eyes on the teacher. He didn't know about Pelly and the other boys, but he nodded his head vigorously. Yes, yes, now he understood.

In the next couple of weeks, Garry talked to Mr. Worthington several times and then went to pray with Rev. Jones, asking God to forgive him of his sins and "receiving" Jesus to be his savior and chief of his life. To Garry's delight, several of the other boys did the same, including Pelly. On June 24, 1827, a procession made its way to the Red River, where Rev. Jones baptized ten boys from the school as new Christians.

After that, Garry's studies took on a different purpose. No longer was he on a quest. He had found the "Leaves of Life," and they had certainly brought him new life and shown him the way to heaven. However, he had much to learn before he was ready to return to his tribe with the prize he had found. Now he had to prepare himself to return to his father and his people.

Garry tried to learn all he could about farming, a skill for improving the daily life of his people. But most of all, he wanted to be able to take back the message of the "Leaves of Life." No longer content to just learn about God from Mr. Worthington and Rev. Jones, Garry learned to read and write. He memorized dozens of Scripture passages and Christian hymns. He learned how to use the Book of Common Prayer for leading daily worship and looked forward to The Day—the day he would be ready to go home.

Three more winters passed. In the spring of 1829, the day finally arrived that Garry and Pelly had worked for so long: graduation day. Each year they had seen other boys graduate and new ones come, but they were still the only ones from the tribes of the Columbia Plateau. Each spring the returning trading brigades had brought reports from the boys' home, but they had been brief and general: "Your father, old Chief Illim, asked about you and said he wants you to study hard and hopes you are well. The salmon run was good this year, but they didn't have so many furs to trade."

Garry was glad for the news, but it didn't tell him much. Mostly he just felt homesick for the next week or two. But now it was graduation time. Soon he and Pelly would be heading home with the outbound brigade.

Mr. Worthington, Rev. Jones, all the students, and even Governor Simpson and a few local families packed into the small schoolhouse for the ceremony on Sunday afternoon, May 10. Rev. Jones opened

with a prayer and Scripture reading, followed by a
short message. Then Mr. Worthington stood up in a
clean white shirt and freshly brushed suit.

"Garry and Pelly, would you please step forward."
Awkwardly folding his hands and looking up at the

roof as though appealing to God sitting there in the rafters, he said, "This is a momentous day. These young men have come farther than any of our other students. They came to find and study what their people call the 'Leaves of Life.'" He looked at Garry. "And what is it your people call God?"

"*Quilent-sat-men*," said Garry.

"Yes," nodded Mr. Worthington, "and it means Creator of All—quite appropriate, I think. Their tribes sent them here to discover the path to God. Well, I can testify that they have found that path through Jesus Christ, and they have come to know Him in a deep and personal way. They have found the path to God, and they are prepared now, after four years of study, to tell others about God and the gift of His Son."

He turned to the table beside him and picked up four books, handing two to Garry and two to Pelly. "On behalf of the Red River Mission of the Church of England, I am presenting each of you with a Holy Bible and a Book of Common Prayer. You are both able to read them now and understand the basics of the Christian faith. We here at the Red River Mission charge you to return to your people with the message of the Gospel. May God go with you!"

Garry and Pelly looked at the two prized books in their hands. What a great gift!

More prayers, hearty congratulations, and a special meal followed the brief ceremony. But for the rest of the afternoon, all Garry could do was open the leather-bound "Leaves of Life" again and again. Not only had he found the prize that his father had sent him to seek, not only had he learned how to read its directions, not only had he studied and memorized many of its secrets—but in his hands he had an actual copy of the "Leaves of Life." He would take it back to his people to show them how to receive God's great gift, thereby fulfilling the old prophecy of Circling Raven.

But first he had to get home. Stepping outside, Garry—four years older and several inches taller than when he had first arrived at the Red River Mission—looked toward the far mountains. Between the mission and home lay 1,850 miles of the most desolate wilderness imaginable.

Chapter 11

The Hard Road Home

Traveling with the next season's outward-bound trappers, Garry and Pelly set off on their long journey. They were no longer the children who had come to the Red River Mission four years earlier but strong young men, returning with the treasure their tribes had entrusted them to find. While at the mission, they had cut their hair and worn the white man's clothing, which was easier to obtain than new buckskin. But Garry was looking forward to the looser, more comfortable clothes of his own people. He would shoot his own deer for soft buckskin and kill a buffalo for a new winter robe.

Garry had not had many occasions to use his prized

rifle while attending school. Much of the game immediately around the fort had been depleted by the farmers along the river. "That is why you must learn to farm," Mr. Worthington had said. "When so many people live in one area and are hunting all the time, they use up the game, so you must learn to grow your own food and raise your own meat."

"All we have to do," Garry had protested, "is move to a new place where the game is plentiful. Three or four years later, we can come back to the old village, and there will be plenty of animals to hunt again."

"That's good," said his teacher. "But what if some other tribe has moved in while you were gone? In fact, what if in every good location you might move to there's already a village set up there? Then you would have to stay put and make the best of where you are. That's when farming would become very valuable. Some day there will be villages in every good valley and at the fork of every beautiful river."

Garry found that hard to believe, but he had applied himself to learning to farm, and now he had a large pouch with pumpkin, corn, beet, parsnip, and bean seeds. He would show his people how to plant them. These vegetables would add some good variety to their diet. But right now, he was looking forward to hunting as much as he wanted.

Travel up Lake Winnipeg was easier than their trip down had been as the boats were equipped with small sails that eased the rowing when the wind came from the right direction. But they did not go all the way to Norway House. It was faster, said the brigade captain, to cut directly west to Grand Rapids when they were three-fourths of the way up the lake. But once they had traveled through Moon Lake and started up the Saskatchewan River, it was hard work all the way with seldom relief provided by the sails.

In spite of how daily hard work with shovels, hoes, and axes had toughened Garry's and Pelly's hands while at school, rowing the heavy boats upstream from dawn until nearly dark day after day soon rubbed through the calluses on their hands. One after the other they tore loose from the boys' palms, leaving bloody patches like coins at the base of each finger. They wrapped their hands with rags, but still the sores oozed from constant work on the oars that jacked the boats slowly up the mighty Saskatchewan River.

The trappers wisely waited until well after the spring floods had subsided before trying to row upstream, but the summer had its own trials in the form of clouds of little black flies that bit and mosquitoes so desperate for a drink of blood that they would dig right through the bear grease Garry smeared on all exposed skin. Some of the trappers who chewed tobacco joked that they were just getting rid of the mosquitoes that had flown in their mouths if anyone complained about their frequent habit of spitting.

Quite an excuse, thought Garry. He had certainly sucked in enough of the noxious bugs that if he had swallowed them he wouldn't need to hunt for meat.

Fort Edmonton again provided a welcome rest for the weary travelers and additional time for Garry's and Pelly's hands to heal. On the river, the open wounds had finally become thick crusts that had slowly turned back to ugly calluses of sorts, except that they seemed to crack and weep and occasionally even bleed a little.

After four days of rest at the fort, the brigade captain said it was time to leave. All the trappers seemed eager to get to their territories. "Got lots o' traps to repair, and I want to set out a new line in the high country above me," said one of the grizzled men dressed head to toe in buckskin. " 'Sides, if I don't get there purty soon, some interloper is likely to horn in on my region."

Garry and Pelly were just as eager to get home, so, tender hands or not, they were ready to hit the trail. Besides, the next leg of the journey would be on horseback rather than rowing a heavy boat upstream.

As they traveled from Fort Edmonton to Fort Assiniboine, Garry recalled that on the eastward journey four years before, he had been so disheartened over the loss of his rifle that he had paid very little attention to where he was going, just followed the horse in front of him. That kind of carelessness in the wilderness could get a person seriously lost. But even though on his first day out he saw few landmarks that he remembered, the trail between the two forts was so well traveled that no one could lose his way.

Most of the trappers had a packhorse in tow, but the boys had all their belongings in rolls carried on their own horses, so the second day out, Garry and Pelly took the lead as the travelers left camp. Garry slung his rifle proudly across his back the way he had so often carried his bow.

They had drifted almost a half a mile ahead of the rest of the party by noon, when the two horses started tossing their heads and prancing sideways. Pelly, followed by Garry, urged the horses forward over a little rise—surprising a huge grizzly bear with two cubs grazing in a huckleberry patch about twenty yards off the trail directly to the right. The bear rose up and grunted while her cubs rambled off away from the travelers.

Pelly tried to keep his frightened horse from bolting as Garry came up behind him. "Just move on slowly," murmured Garry softly. "She's not likely to attack the two of us, especially when we're on horseback."

"Oh, yeah?" muttered Pelly, eyeing the protective mother bear swaying from side to side.

The grizzly roared, dropped to all fours, and suddenly charged the boys. She skidded to a stop in a cloud of dust about ten yards away, proving it was only a bluff, but not before Pelly's horse had bolted up the trail at a full gallop. With all his might, Garry held his horse steady as it pranced and snorted and

twisted in place. The bear, however, took off in a full run after Pelly.

Garry let his horse go but had to fight to keep her

on the trail. His mare also wanted to run, but in the opposite direction. "Hi-eee! Hi-eee!" yelled Garry, trying to distract the bear as he followed along.

In spite of the fall that had broken the leg of the governor's horse, Garry had always considered himself an excellent horseman, able to control an animal in almost any situation, but getting a shy horse to race after an angry grizzly bear along a rugged, twisting trail was almost impossible. Ahead Garry could see that Pelly wasn't having it any easier even though his horse was fleeing the bear.

Garry saw Pelly yank his horse hard to the left and realized that the trail had come up on a ravine, threading its way along the lip before descending a narrow path to the creek thirty feet below. Garry watched in horror as Pelly's horse slipped and tumbled with him down the bank.

The bear didn't even wait for the dust to settle before it started picking its way down the steep bank. Garry skidded to a stop at the top and hopped off his horse while at the same time pulling his rifle from his back. He took a stance and raised it to his shoulder just as he saw Pelly's horse scramble to its feet and run off down the creek, but the bear was still working her way down to where Pelly lay against a huge boulder.

Should he shoot? Could one shot drop an animal that huge? What if he missed and hit Pelly? But there was no time to waste. He squeezed the trigger and . . . nothing. Frantically he pulled back the hammer and let it fall again. Still nothing, and the bear was getting closer to Pelly!

And then Garry saw the problem. Somehow, his flint had been knocked to the side in the hammer and wasn't striking the frizzen. He adjusted it, pulled the hammer back, aimed, and squeezed the trigger again. The gun roared, and when the smoke cleared, the bear was running up the creek. Had he wounded her? Had he missed? It didn't matter. The old gal was leaving, and Pelly was safe.

Garry hopped and stumbled his way down the bank, kicking up little slides of dust and gravel wherever he landed, until he was at the bottom.

"Pelly! Pelly, are you okay? She didn't get you, did she?"

Pelly groaned and tried to sit up, but with a cry of pain slumped back, his head resting on the boulder. As though pulling his lips to the sides with his fingers, he exposed his gritted teeth and groaned again. Then he coughed.

"Stay still. Let me help you," said Garry as he kneeled beside his friend.

Slowly Garry was able to get Pelly into a sitting position, then standing, then slowly walking down the gully to where the trail crossed. Occasionally Pelly coughed and spat up a little blood, but his shoulder was causing the greatest pain. Garry could hardly touch his friend's arm without him crying out in pain.

In a few minutes the other trappers caught up and were ambling down the steep trail into the ravine. "Where are your horses?" one of them called.

Hearing the story about the bear, the man nodded. "Figures. My horse has been wanting to jump out from under me. Musta smelled that old bruin." He dismounted and came over to Pelly. "Here. Let me see that arm."

He touched it gently, glancing up at Pelly's face when the boy grimaced in pain.

"Hmm. Dislocated your shoulder. Here, Garry, you get around behind him like this, and hold him firmly."

Garry was no sooner in position than the trapper grabbed Pelly's lame arm and gave a yank and twist. Pelly screamed in pain and then let out a sigh of relief. It had worked. Pelly's shoulder was back in place, and though it was still extremely sore, they could tell from his face that the stabbing pain was gone.

The other trappers helped the boys retrieve their runaway horses, and within a half hour, they were on their way again. But as they rode, Pelly continued coughing and spitting up blood. "That don't sound good to me," said the trapper who had popped Pelly's shoulder back in place. "You might have broke a rib and punctured your lung!"

By the time they arrived at Fort Assiniboine that evening, Pelly had such a high fever that he seemed delirious, and he could hardly stay on his horse.

"Take him into my house," ordered Captain McKay, the man in charge of the fort. "There's a little room in the back he can use."

✧ ✧ ✧

Garry stayed with Pelly every minute during the next three days as his friend slipped in and out of consciousness. The stuffy little room smelled of camphor from some salve Captain McKay said would help him breath. Garry felt he might do better if he got out into some fresh air, but any attempt to move him threw Pelly into a dreadful coughing fit.

Just before dawn on the fourth day, Garry woke from dozing beside Pelly's bed and noticed something funny about Pelly's breathing. The intervals were too long.

"Pelly?" Garry held his own breath, waiting, praying to see Pelly's chest rise one more time in the dim light of the candle. Seconds dragged into a minute. "Pelly!" He shook his friend, longing to hear the rasping wheeze that had become so frightening during the recent hours. "Pelly, wake up! You can't do this! Breathe! Breathe!"

But Pelly's breath never came again.

Garry's legs felt like angleworms, slowly giving way and sinking to the floor as darkness began to creep in from the sides to choke out his vision. His head and arms draped over the bed like melting wax. Pelly was dead! Dead! Garry couldn't move.

Why! Why had he died? If God had wanted them to bring the Leaves of Life and its message about Jesus back to their people, why had God allowed him to die? Pelly had spent four years studying and learning about God . . . but for what?

Apparently Garry's moans attracted the attention

of Captain McKay, who appeared in the doorway. "Is he gone?"

Garry nodded, choking back the tears. But he didn't get up.

"I'm sorry, son. I—I'll get some of the Indian women outside to bury him."

"No." Garry pushed himself to his feet. "He must have a Christian burial. He was a Christian and . . . the best friend I ever had."

"But . . . but we don't have nobody here to pray for him or nothin'," mumbled the deep voice of the captain.

Garry looked at the man who stood there in his worn-out long underwear. What was with these white people who didn't even know Jesus? "Don't need anybody else. I can pray well enough."

McKay nodded, his bushy black beard bobbing like a leaf in the breeze. "Good enough, then. I'll find someone to dig a grave and fashion a wooden cross for him."

"Thank you," said Garry, numbly turning back to his friend.

Only a half dozen people gathered around the gravesite that afternoon as they lowered Pelly's body, wrapped in his Hudson's Bay Company blanket, into the hole. Captain McKay had suggested that possibly the blanket could be of more value if given to his family, but Garry insisted that his friend's body needed to be treated with some dignity.

It was only after the brief service that Garry discovered why the trappers with whom they had traveled all the way from Fort Gibraltar were not present at the funeral. "Oh, they headed on up country while you were nursing your friend," said the captain. "There was no way to keep them here for long."

It took a moment for his words to sink in. Pelly was dead. His traveling companions were gone. He was alone. Steeling his voice to keep it steady, he said, "Guess I'll be heading out on my own, then. I'll get started in the morning."

"Ah . . . can't let you do that," said the captain.

"Why not? I can find my way up the Athabasca to Jasper House. Maybe I'll meet up with the brigade. If not . . . I know the way over the pass and down the Columbia."

"It's not that," said the captain. "Some of the trappers told me that Governor Simpson is very concerned about the safety and welfare of you boys. Apparently the governor is concerned that if one of you should die, it might start an uprising among the plateau tribes. They said I should keep you here until he comes out himself to escort you home."

A knot formed in Garry's stomach. "When will that be?"

"Well, no way of knowing. If he doesn't travel with the brigade, he sometimes comes in the fall before the snow flies. On the other hand, he doesn't make the trip every year."

"What? I can't stay here indefinitely! That's like keeping me in jail!"

The captain shrugged. "Sorry, son. But I can't go against the governor's wishes."

Chapter 12

Back Up Mount Spokane

After Pelly's burial, the captain assigned Garry to the bunkhouse where a couple of other men who helped run the fort slept. Garry said nothing, but he wasn't going to remain trapped in Fort Assiniboine— not if he could help it. He had to get home. He had been sent on a mission, and if Pelly couldn't return with him to complete it, he would have to do it by himself. He certainly wasn't going to wait months or a year for the governor to arrive. The sooner he could get home, the better.

That night, Garry waited until all was quiet and the fires had burned low before he slipped out of his bunk. Stuffing the hard bread and dried meat he'd saved from his supper into the bag containing his books, seeds, and blanket, he slung the bag over his shoulders and let himself quietly out of the bunkhouse, careful not to wake the other men.

He was heading for the gate of the fort when he remembered his rifle. He had been in school so long that he had gotten out of the habit of keeping his weapons near him at all times. How foolish! He had left his rifle in the little room in the captain's house next to the bed where Pelly died. Worse, he had since learned that it had been the captain's bed, which he had graciously loaned to the injured Pelly.

Making his way by nothing but the light of the stars, Garry diverted his path to the captain's house and gently tried the door. But it was bolted from the inside. He went around to the side and was ready to slit the greased window skin when he heard the captain cough and get up out of bed. Garry waited, but then he saw a light flare up from a lamp or candle.

There was no retrieving his gun now. Who knew how long the captain would remain awake. It was either wait for some other night to escape or go without his rifle.

That rifle meant so much to him—a prize in itself and earned the hard way—but he decided that his freedom and completing his mission meant more than the gun. He turned away and headed toward the gates.

Once outside, he could not replace the pole that bolted the gates closed from the inside, so he propped a large rock against them to prevent them from swinging open with the wind and possibly making enough noise to set off an alarm before he escaped.

As he headed down to the river's edge, a dog began barking from one of the tepees outside the fort. The mutt came racing toward him, yapping all the while but remaining just far enough away that Garry could not catch it and calm it.

Garry continued down the path, hoping the dog would give up and go home, but apparently it considered this whole area its territory and Garry an intruder. At the water's edge Garry found only two canoes—a large one that would require two or three people to paddle it against the current and a small one, old and half full of water. He emptied the water while the dog continued to bark and was about to push it out into the current when someone began calling for the dog. Soon a light flared near the tepees. Garry could see an old woman had ignited a grass torch from the dying coals of the evening's fire.

She stumbled toward the river, calling and scolding the dog. A layer of clouds hid the moon; Garry hoped that the old woman couldn't see him with her own eyes dimmed by the brilliance of the torch light, but he didn't want to take any chances. He tossed a stick at the dog, hoping to chase it away, and stepped into the large canoe, where he lay down on the bottom, out of sight.

Unsure whether to return to the woman or continue chasing off "the intruder," the dog ran toward the woman and then back to the canoes, then back to the woman. Garry peeked over the gunwale of the canoe and sighed with relief when he saw her reach down quicker than any old woman should move and grab the dog by the scruff of the neck as it came close to her.

The dog let out one yelp, then followed her obediently up toward the tepees.

A few moments later, Garry was on his way upriver in the smaller, leaky canoe. But at least he was no longer trapped in the fort!

The hardest part of the canoe trip was passing the place where he had dived for his rifle, where Pelly had hauled him from the water. A deep sense of loss threatened to overwhelm him. He was returning home without his rifle . . . and without Pelly. He coasted on the dark water, almost tempted to dive in again as though he might find what he had lost in those cold depths. But he knew that wasn't true. And he did have the Leaves of Life and good news for his people.

That would have to be enough.

Late that night he beached the canoe some distance from Jasper House and hiked around it, keeping hidden in the woods lest some Hudson's Bay Company men see him and try to detain him. He slept in the hollow of an immense rotting pine near the point where the trail began to ascend toward Athabasca Pass.

The next morning it wasn't hard to follow the trail on foot, and soon fresh footprints in the snow proved that the trappers had gone that way within the last few days. The bread and dried meat were gone; all

Garry could do was quench his thirst with snow.

He hadn't thought about how he would navigate the Columbia. When he reached the river on the other side of the pass, he realized no riverboats were waiting for him. Upset with himself for not having foreseen this, Garry began hiking, unwilling to let anything stop him.

At the end of one day's hiking, he had traveled south, west, and then had to loop back east without finding any way to hike down the Columbia. What he had failed to realize was that at that point the Columbia River, its tributaries, and Kinbasket Lake created a tangle of waterways that were impossible to cross without a boat of some kind.

With great relief he finally stumbled upon a tribe of Indians he did not recognize. They were camped on the banks of the big river, and he gratefully accepted their offer of food. As he filled his belly with hot venison stew, Garry listened carefully but couldn't understand a word of their language. He tried sign language, but it took over an hour of bartering before he finally reached a deal to trade his Hudson's Bay blanket for an old canoe.

Again he was on his journey.

The long summer days provided sixteen hours of daylight, and Garry took advantage of every one of them to paddle down the mighty Columbia, sometimes plowing through its smooth waters, amazed at the towering saw-toothed mountains rising to the sky, and sometimes bobbing like a leaf over the rough rapids and huge waves, never sure whether

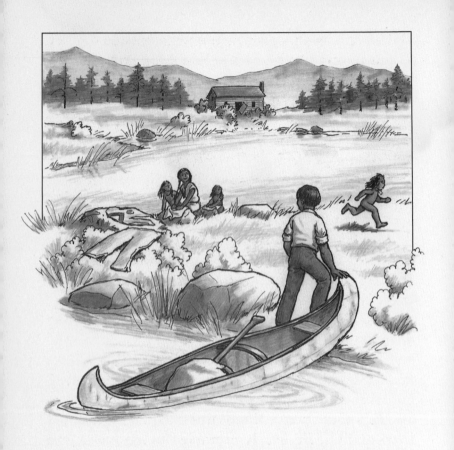

the next toss of the boiling water would capsize him or not.

Four exhausting days later, with nothing to eat but some of the pumpkin seeds he had intended for planting, Garry paddled his leaky canoe ashore along the Spokane River, with the lodges of his village in sight across the green meadow where horses grazed peacefully in the late afternoon. Across the river, Spokane House looked abandoned, its door hanging open and blackberry bushes growing all around.

The children playing at the water's edge did not recognize him. And it was only after staring at him for several moments that his sister, Qunit-qua-apee, who was washing clothes in the river, squealed and ran toward him with her arms wide. "Garry! Garry is back! Garry is finally back!" Then to one of the children, who were now staring open-mouthed at Garry, she said, "Go tell your Uncle Sulz-lee that his brother is here. Go on! Hurry up! And tell everyone," she called after the naked child who was running across the grass toward the village.

Soon a stream of people were running from the village to meet him as he walked beside his sister through the meadow in the lengthening shadows. He spotted his brother and other familiar faces. "But where is my father? I don't see Chief Illim."

His sister dropped her head. "You didn't hear? He died winter before last. But his passing was peaceful."

Garry felt as if one of the snowfields clinging to the sides of the Rocky Mountains had just avalanched down on him. He nearly crumbled to his knees and couldn't catch his breath. After all the miles . . . the long, dark winters . . . the hard study . . . and the death of Pelly . . . this was too much. His father had sent him to bring back the Leaves of Life, but he was too late. He would not be able to tell his father about God's gift of His Son, Jesus. What would happen to the old chief in the afterlife?

The images of his brother and the other villagers coming toward him across the meadow swirled before his eyes. Soon they were all around him, slapping him on the back, pulling at his short hair, and laughing good-naturedly about his strange clothes. The old women were looking up at him and marveling at how tall and strong he had grown. But Garry felt as though he were inside a cocoon with the hubbub spinning around him on the other side of a thin shell.

No one understood. He had failed his mission. His father was dead. He was alone.

Garry let the crowd move him along toward the village, like a log floating down the river when the ice breaks up in the spring, being jostled this way and that but unable to affect his destination.

When the sun had set and he was seated with his brother and some of the tribal elders around the fire as the women stood behind them whispering in little huddles, his brother Sultz-lee said, "Did the white men freeze your tongue? You've hardly said a handful of words since you got home. What's the matter? Did you get the Leaves of Life? Father always wanted to know."

Garry nodded. "Yes, I got them."

"Well, then! Tomorrow we will send out messengers to all the Spokane villages and to the Nez Perce and the Flathead—to everyone!—and invite them all to a great potlatch."

"A potlatch?" said Garry, realizing for the first time what his brother was saying. "I have nothing to give them. Why would we have a potlatch?"

Sulz-lee frowned, confused. "You said you brought back the Leaves of Life. You can give them the words from it. What could be more valuable to give away than the secret path to heaven? It will be the greatest potlatch ever."

Garry said nothing. Why did his heart feel so heavy?

Garry arose early the next morning and left the village before dawn. He took the Leaves of Life bound in brown leather and climbed the rocky paths of Mount Spokane to one of his old favorite spots overlooking the valley. He tried to pray as the rising sun awoke the valleys below to dazzling color. Why had God brought him all this way if his father was not here to receive the Bible and recommend his message to the tribe? Even worse, what joy could he convey in telling the Gospel if his father had gone to the place of separation and suffering rather than to God's side in heaven?

Desperate for answers, he opened his Bible and began reading the same passage in Romans 1 that Mr. Worthington taught from: "Because that which may be known of God is manifest in them; for God hath shewed it unto them. For the invisible things of him from the creation of the world are clearly seen, being understood by the things that are made, even his eternal power and Godhead."

If his father had worshiped the true God from what he learned in nature as Garry knew he had, and if God had sent his people the prophecy about the Leaves of Life, why hadn't God kept his father alive long enough to receive the gift of Jesus Christ?

How unfair to take him just before the message arrived! It seemed unjust!

Just? Unjust? From somewhere Garry remembered verses about God being just. But where? He turned to the back of the Bible, knowing that the Book of Revelation spoke of final judgments and how everything would end. Though he had not been able to understand what he read there, this time as he thumbed through the pages, his eyes fell on verse 3 of chapter 15: "Great and marvellous are thy works, Lord God Almighty; just and true are thy ways, thou King of saints."

" 'Just and true are thy ways. Just and true are thy ways. Just and true are thy ways.' " Garry kept saying it over and over. His father had longed to know about the true God. If God was indeed just, then He would deal fairly with his father.

But how could he know? How could he know exactly what his father faced in the afterlife?

Slowly a peace settled on him and lifted the heaviness in his heart. Just like everything else he had learned about *Quilent-sat-men*—Creator of All— Garry would have to practice faith by trusting that God would deal justly with his father, whatever that meant. Yes. He could do that. If he could trust God with his own future, he could trust God with his father's life in the afterlife.

A large black raven landed on a boulder behind Garry and began cawing in its irritating voice as though trying to chase him away. Garry smiled, recalling the vision Circling Raven had received on that very mountain and God's instruction to pay attention to the marks on the Leaves of Life.

He stood up and waved his arm to scare away the black bird cawing off-key, which sailed off over the valley below. Then in a clear voice that floated after the bird, Garry began to sing his favorite song he had learned at the mission:

> I am so glad that our Father in heaven
> Tells of His love in the book he has given
> Wonderful things in the Bible I see
> This is the dearest that Jesus loves me.
> > Jesus loves me
> > O Jesus loves me
> > Jesus loves even me.

When the echo of soft notes had floated away after the receding raven, Garry sighed and started down the mountain. He had indeed brought home Good News for his people.

More About Chief Spokane Garry

Spokane Garry became a great evangelist, and in years to follow, his people honored him as an important chief. Hundreds traveled from all over the region to hear him preach from the Leaves of Life about the path to heaven through Jesus Christ. He taught them songs of worship and instructed them to pray morning and evening and observe the Ten Commandments. He taught the people to set aside Sunday for worship and learning about God. He also instructed them in basic farming techniques.

Within four years, the impact of his preaching had spread throughout the whole region, even as far as Fort Alexandria, British Columbia, over four hundred miles to the northwest in Canada.

But perhaps the greatest testimony to the effectiveness of this revival occurred the year after Garry's return, when five regional chiefs brought their sons and asked Garry to take them to the mission school so they could learn the Good News, as well. The Nez Perce tribe also sent a delegation down to St. Louis, asking for a missionary. In 1836, Marcus and Narcissa Whitman and Henry and Eliza Spalding responded to that call . . . with mixed results. But that's another story that can be read in the TRAILBLAZER BOOK *Attack in the Rye Grass.*

In the village across the river from the abandoned Spokane House, Garry built a small church, complete with a bell, where he called his tribe together on Sundays for worship. On weekdays Garry held school in the little building, where he taught English, simple agriculture (growing potatoes and vegetables), and the Christian life. During the winter, when the tribe was not busy hunting and gathering, he had as many as a hundred adults and children in attendance at his school.

By the fall of 1833, all but one of the other students Garry had sent to the Red River Mission had graduated and returned to teach Christianity to their people.

In the summer of 1834, Captain Bonneville made a trip through the region and recorded the following in Washington Irving's 1837 book, *Adventures of Captain Bonneville*:

Sunday is invariably kept sacred among these

tribes. They will not raise [move] their camp on that day unless in extreme cases of danger or hunger; neither will they hunt, nor fish, nor trade, nor perform any kind of labor on that day. A part of it is passed in prayer and religious ceremonies. Some chief... assembles the community. After invoking blessings from the Deity, he addresses the assemblage, exhorting them to good conduct, to be diligent in providing for their families, to abstain from lying and stealing, to avoid quarreling or cheating in their play, to be just and hospitable to all strangers who may be among them. Prayers and exhortations are also made early in the morning on weekdays.

Undoubtedly, by the time these religious practices had spread from village to village and tribe to tribe, they lacked some of the essential content of the Gospel, but they nevertheless reflected a people eager to know and serve God.

On this foundation, Garry and the other students from the Red River Mission begged the Church of England to send them missionaries who could build a strong, sound church among them. But for a variety of reasons, years passed without a missionary.

Finally, in 1835, the American Board of Foreign Missions sent Rev. Samuel Parker to survey the region. Upon arriving in a Nez Perce village, the chief agreed to assemble all the people for worship the next day, which was Sunday, September 6.

Parker was amazed when four to five hundred men, women, and children gathered in a carefully prepared lodge about a hundred feet long and twenty feet wide. He reported, "The whole sight affected me, and filled me with admiration, and I felt as though it was the house of God and the gate of heaven." They sang and prayed and listened to Parker's sermon, translated by an interpreter from Fort Hall, at the end of which they said in unison their equivalent of *amen*.

The next summer, Henry and Eliza Spalding came as missionaries to the Nez Perce while Marcus and Narcissa Whitman went to the neighboring Cayuse.

Soon, however, large numbers of white settlers began to arrive, aided considerably by the Whitmans' efforts in "opening" the Oregon Trail. From then on, friction with white settlers hindered the establishment of a solid church.

The massacre at the Whitman mission in 1847 sealed in the minds of many white settlers that Native Americans were their enemies—or at the very least obstacles to their desire for land—and so increasing pressure was mounted to remove the Indians to reservations.

Bloody skirmishes and all-out war ensued for years. In 1855, Chief Garry met with white representatives in an appeal for understanding and peace. That same year, Old Joseph, chief of the Nez Perce, signed a treaty with the U.S. that allowed his people to retain much of their traditional lands. However, eight years later, another treaty was drafted that severely reduced the amount of land, but Old Joseph maintained that this second treaty was never agreed to by his people. And so it went.

By 1870, Chief Garry realized that all the tension and lack of receiving missionaries to build a church for the Spokane had left his people in moral decay—marriages failing when white husbands deserted Indian wives, alcoholism from the whiskey introduced by the whites, and a general disinterest in the things of God.

Along with two assistants, Chief Garry launched a revival among his people in 1871 and experienced substantial success, so much so that he wrote to Henry Spalding, asking him if he would come and help. Accompanied by fourteen Nez Perce believers, Spalding held three weeks of services in May 1873 and then two additional evangelistic trips later that summer. At the end of the revival, heralded by the theme, "What shall we do to be saved?" 334 people on examination gave satisfactory evidence of conversion and were baptized, including 81 children, according to Thomas Jessett in his book, *Chief Spokane Garry: Christian, Statesman and Friend of the Whiteman*.

But still no permanent minister was assigned to minister among the Spokane. Not until 1884, fifty-five years after Garry returned from the Red River Mission to plant the seed, was Rev. J. Compton Burnett sent by the Episcopal Church (as the Church of England was called in the United States) to Spokane Falls. Unfortunately he proved to be an unscrupulous man, who swindled the tribe out of land for his own farming ambitions.

After this, Chief Garry never again asked the Episcopal Church for assistance.

Chief Garry recalled the last half of old Circling Raven's prophecy: "After the white men with the Leaves of Life come, other white men will come who will make slaves of us. Then our world will end . . . . We will simply be overrun by the white men as though by grasshoppers. When this happens, we should not fight, as it would only create unnecessary bloodshed." Certainly this tragedy was coming true for all Indian peoples. Garry could not stop it! On three occasions, he applied for a reservation along the Spokane River where his people could "work the land and practice the teachings of Jesus Christ." But the land was too valuable to the white settlers, and each time the U.S. government denied his request, saying the Spokane would have to remove themselves to the Colville, Coeur d'Alene, or Jacko Reservations.

Finally Garry himself was swindled out of his little farm. In 1891, he became too ill to work, and when a deceitful white man promised that if Garry would pay five dollars and sign some papers, he could get Garry's farm back for him, Garry said, "I am dying, and all I am thinking of is God. Soon I'll have nothing more to do with this world."

With his well-worn Bible and prayer book in his hands, Chief Spokane Garry died in his sleep on January 14, 1892.

Such sad conduct on the part of our government and even the church begs for some kind of a response. Fortunately the Bible gives us four steps for dealing with such sweeping historical wrongs as the ill-treatment of Native Americans or the enslavement of Africans. (1) Acknowledge it was wrong. (2) Clearly ask for forgiveness. (3) Do no further wrong. (4) Be prepared to do whatever you can to make it right.

The Bible says, "Confess your sins" (James 5:16). Too often we are tempted to excuse or explain away past wrongs by saying things like, "Well, the other side wasn't perfect, either," or "That's just the way it was back then." Perhaps we make these excuses because we find the burden of guilt too heavy. It is hard to say that in the process of building this great country, our forebears did wrong. It makes us feel like we don't deserve our current privileges and wealth. And on one hand, we don't. Everything we have has come from someone else, even our most prized possession, eternal life.

But God doesn't leave us feeling guilty. We can ask forgiveness. "But," you may say, "why should *I* ask forgiveness? I didn't do the wrong." Hopefully not, but if you consider yourself an American, then you identify with and benefit from this country's history. The Bible includes examples of "innocent" people asking forgiveness on behalf of the guilty. Jesus Christ prayed on the cross, "Father, forgive them, for they know not what they do." But long before that Nehemiah prayed, "[I] confess the sins of the children of Israel, which we have sinned against thee: both I and my father's house have sinned" (Nehemiah 1:6), even though it was unlikely that he personally committed the sins he then lists. So we *can* and *should* ask God's forgiveness for past wrongs even if we didn't personally commit them. And, if we are ever in a position where it is appropriate, we can ask individuals for forgiveness for how our ancestors treated them or their ancestors.

Doing no further wrong is self-explanatory, but the fourth step may be more challenging. There may come times and ways when we can and should make restitution for those wrongs, even the wrongs done by our ancestors. After all, most of us are still enjoying land that was obtained unfairly from the Indians and wealth that came from the unpaid efforts of slaves. We owe a lot. How to repay what was unfairly taken is a complicated issue, but the *willingness* to "make it right" is a godly attitude.

For Further Reading

Jessett, Thomas E. *Chief Spokan Garry*. Minneapolis, Minn.: T.S. Denison & Company, Inc., 1960.
Twiss, Richard. *One Church, Many Tribes*. Ventura, Calif.: Regal, 2000.

STORIES

WORTH TELLING!

Delight in the Dramatic Stories from Lives of Christian Heroes

Every *Hero Tales* book is a beautifully illustrated collection of exciting and inspirational readings. Courage, faith, perseverance, mercy, and many more godly characteristics are revealed in the lives of men and women in every era of history. These books will encourage everyone in the family to live more fully for Jesus.

Hero Tales: Volume I
Includes: Amy Carmichael, Harriet Tubman, Samuel Morris, and more!

Hero Tales: Volume III
Includes: Billy Graham, Mother Theresa, Brother Andrew, and more!

Hero Tales: Volume II
Includes: Corrie ten Boom, Florence Nightingale, Jim Elliot, and others!

Hero Tales: Volume IV
Includes: C.S. Lewis, Joy Ridderhof, Ben Carson, and more!

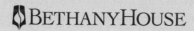